'Perhaps you won't be in such a hurry to leave if I tell you that I have a d___ in m___ that I'd like to talk ___ ___ ___ ___l that would b___ ___ ___ s well as yours___ ___ ___lmly.

Riveted, Natalie immediately pulled her hand away from th___ ___ doorknob and turned to face him.

'What kind ___

Pacing a lit___ ___ ___ thoughts, Ludo took his tim___ ___ ___topped pacing to settle his g___ ___ ___quisitive face in front of hi___

'I will in___ ___ or your father's business ___ ___ in if you agree to come wit___ ___ ___ay the role of my fiancée.'

Natalie ___ ___tue, her stunned express___ ___ ___sn't entirely sure she'd ___ ___ ___oved across the room ___ ___ed wing-backed armch___ ___ into it.

When ___ ___ to meet his eyes Ludo ex___ ___ate moment of undeniabl___ ___ ___ he suddenly knew she was g___ ___ ___ ___ offer.

The day **Maggie Cox** saw the film version of *Wuthering Heights*, with a beautiful Merle Oberon and a very handsome Laurence Olivier, was the day she became hooked on romance. From that day onwards she spent a lot of time dreaming up her own romances, secretly hoping that one day she might become published and get paid for doing what she loved most! Now that her dream is being realised, she wakes up every morning and counts her blessings. She is married to a gorgeous man, and is the mother of two wonderful sons. Her two other great passions in life—besides her family and reading/writing—are music and films.

Recent titles by the same author:

WHAT HIS MONEY CAN'T HIDE
DISTRACTED BY HER VIRTUE
A DEVILISHLY DARK DEAL
THE LOST WIFE

IN PETRAKIS'S POWER

BY
MAGGIE COX

First published in Great Britain 2013
by Mills & Boon, an imprint of Harlequin (UK) Limited.
Harlequin (UK) Limited, Eton House, 18-24 Paradise Road,
Richmond, Surrey TW9 1SR

© Maggie Cox 2013

ISBN: 978 0 263 90027 9

Harlequin (UK) policy is to use papers that are natural, renewable
and recyclable products and made from wood grown in sustainable
forests. The logging and manufacturing process conform to the
legal environmental regulations of the country of origin.

Printed and bound in Spain
by Blackprint CPI, Barcelona

IN PETRAKIS'S
POWER

CHAPTER ONE

'TICKETS, PLEASE.'

Having just dropped down into her seat after a mad dash to catch the train, flustered and hot, Natalie Carr delved into her voluminous red leather bag and unzipped an inside compartment to retrieve her ticket. The discovery that it was nowhere to be seen was akin to the jolting shock of tumbling down an entire flight of stairs. With her heartbeat hammering in her chest, she raised her head to proffer an apologetic smile to the guard.

'Sorry…I know it's here somewhere…'

But it wasn't. Desperately trying to recall her last-minute trip to the ladies' before running onto the platform to catch the train, she had a horrible feeling that after checking her seat number she'd left the ticket, in its official first-class sleeve, on the glass shelf beneath the mirror, when she'd paused to retouch her lipstick.

Feeling slightly queasy as a further search through her bag failed to yield it, she exhaled a frustrated sigh. 'I'm afraid it looks like I've lost my ticket. I stopped off at the ladies' just before boarding the train and I think I might have accidentally left it in there. If the train weren't already moving I'd go back and look for it.'

'I'm sorry, miss, but I'm afraid that unless you pay for another ticket you'll have to get off at the next stop. You'll also have to pay for the fare there.'

The officious tone used by the florid and grey-haired train guard conveyed unequivocally that he wouldn't be open to any pleas for understanding. Natalie wished that she'd had the presence of mind to bring some extra cash with her, but she hadn't. Her father had sent her the ticket out of the blue, along with an unsettling note that had practically begged her not to 'desert him' in his 'hour of need', and it had sent her into a spin. Consequently, she'd absent-mindedly grabbed a purse that contained only some loose change instead of the wallet that housed her credit card.

'But I can't get off at the next stop. It's very important that I get to London today. Could you take my name and address and let me send you the money for the ticket when I get back home?'

'I'm afraid it's company policy that—'

'I'll pay for the lady's ticket. Was it a return?'

For the first time she noticed the only other passenger in the compartment. He was sitting in a seat at a table on the opposite side of the aisle. Even though she'd flown into a panic at losing her ticket, she couldn't believe she hadn't noticed him straight away. If the arresting scent of his expensive cologne didn't immediately distinguish him as a man of substantial means and impeccable good taste, the flawless dark grey pinstriped suit that looked as if it came straight out of an Armani showroom certainly did.

Even without those compelling assets, his appearance

was striking. Along with blond hair that had a fetching kink in it, skin that was sun-kissed and golden, and light sapphire eyes that could surely corner the market in sizzling intensity, a dimple in his chin set a provocative seal on the man's undoubted sex appeal. Staring back into that sculpted visage was like having a private viewing of the most sublime portrait by one of the great masters.

A wave of heat that felt shockingly and disturbingly intimate made Natalie clench every muscle in her body. If she hadn't already been on her guard, she certainly was now. She didn't know this man from Adam, *or* his motive for offering to pay for her ticket, and she quickly reminded herself that the newspapers were full of stomach-churning stories about gullible women being duped by supposedly 'respectable' men.

'That's a very kind offer but I couldn't possibly accept it...I don't even know you.'

In a cultured voice, with a trace of an accent she couldn't quite place, the stranger replied, 'Let me get the matter of a replacement ticket out of the way. Then I will introduce myself.'

'But I can't let you pay for my ticket...I really can't.'

'You have already stated that it is very important you get to London today. Is it wise to refuse help when it is offered?'

There was no doubt she was in a fix and the handsome stranger knew it. But Natalie still resisted. 'Yes, I do need to get to London. But you don't know me and I don't know you.'

'You are wary of trusting me, perhaps?'

His somewhat amused smile made her feel even more gauche than she felt already.

'Do you want a ticket or not, madam?' The guard was understandably exasperated with her procrastination.

'I don't think I—'

'The lady would most definitely like a ticket. Thank you,' the stranger immediately interjected.

Her protest had clearly landed on deaf ears. Not only did he have the chiselled good looks of a modern-day Adonis, the timbre of the man's voice was like burnished oak—smoky, compelling, and undeniably sexy. Natalie found her previous resolve to be careful dangerously weakening.

'Okay…if you're sure?'

Her need to get to London was paramount, and it overrode her reservations. Besides, her instinct told her the man was being utterly genuine and didn't pose any kind of threat. She prayed it was a good instinct. Meanwhile the train guard was staring at them in obvious bewilderment, as though wondering why this handsome, well-heeled male passenger would *insist* on paying for a complete stranger's ticket. After all, with her bohemian clothing, casually dried long brown hair with now fading blonde highlights, and not much make-up to speak of, she knew she wasn't the kind of 'high-maintenance' woman who would attract a man as well-groomed and wealthy as the golden-haired male sitting opposite her. But if the smoky-coloured pencil she'd used to underline her big grey eyes with helped create the illusion that she was more attractive than she was, then at that moment Natalie was grateful for the ruse. For she knew she had no choice but to accept the man's kindness. It was vital that she met up with her dad.

She could hardly shake the memory of his distressed tone when she'd rung him to confirm that she'd received the train ticket and once again he'd reiterated his urgent need to see her. It was so unlike him to admit to a human need, and it suggested he was just as fallible and fragile as anyone else—she had guessed all along that he was. Once, long ago, she had heard her mother angrily accuse him of being incapable of loving or needing anyone. His business and the drive to expand his bank account was the real love of his life, she'd cried, and Natalie didn't doubt his obsessive single-mindedness had been a huge factor in their break-up.

When, after their divorce, her mother made the decision to return to Hampshire, where she had spent much of her youth, Natalie, then sixteen, had elected to go with her. As much as she'd loved her dad, and known him to be charming and affable, Natalie had also known he was far too unreliable and unpredictable to share a home with. But in recent years, after visiting him as often as she could manage, she'd become convinced that in his heart he knew money was no substitute for not having someone he loved close by.

From time to time she'd seen loneliness and regret in his eyes at being separated from his family. His tendency to try to compensate for the pain it caused him by regularly entertaining the company of young attractive women was clearly not helping to make him any happier. Several of her visits over the past two years had confirmed that. He seemed disgruntled with everything…

even the phenomenally successful chain of small bijou hotels that had made him his fortune.

'I just need a single,' she told the arresting stranger, who didn't seem remotely perturbed that she'd taken so long to make up her mind about whether to accept his offer or not. 'And it doesn't have to be in first class. My dad sent me the ticket, but I'm quite happy to travel as I usually do in second.'

She couldn't disguise her awkwardness and embarrassment as she watched the man hand his credit card over to the guard. She felt even more awkward when he deliberately ignored her assertion and went ahead and requested a first-class ticket. Natalie hoped to God he believed her explanation about her dad sending her the ticket. After all, she was sure she didn't resemble a typical first-class passenger.

Trust her dad to unwittingly add to her discomfort by making such a needlessly overblown gesture. He always travelled first class himself, which was why he'd automatically paid for his daughter to do the same. Now she really wished he hadn't.

When the satisfied train guard had sorted out the necessary ticket, then wished them both an enjoyable journey, the impeccably dressed stranger handed it over to her and smiled. Natalie was very glad that the compartment was occupied by just the two of them right then, because if anyone else had witnessed the man's astonishing act of chivalry she would have wanted the floor to open up and swallow her.

Accepting the ticket as her face flooded with heat, she prayed her see-sawing emotions would very soon calm down. 'This is so kind of you…thank you…thank you so much.'

'It is my pleasure.'

'Will you write down your name and address for me so that I can send you what I owe you?' She was already rummaging in her voluminous red leather tote for a pen and notepad.

'We will have plenty of time for that. Why don't we sort it out when we get to London?'

Lost for words, and somewhat exhausted by her growing tension, Natalie lowered her bag onto the seat next to her by the window and exhaled a heavy sigh.

With a disarming smile, her companion suggested, 'Why don't we help ease any awkwardness between us by introducing ourselves?'

'All right, then. My name is Natalie.'

It was a mystery to her why she didn't give him her full name. The thought that it was because she was momentarily dazzled by his good looks hardly pleased her. What did she think she was playing at? How often had she groaned at a friend who seemed to lose every ounce of common sense whenever a fit, handsome man engaged her in conversation and became convinced he must think her the most beautiful girl in the world? Such embarrassing silliness was not for her. She'd rather stay single for the rest of her natural life than delude herself that she was something that she wasn't….

'And I am Ludovic…but my family and friends call me Ludo.'

She frowned, 'Ludovic? How unusual.'

'It's a family name.' Beneath his immaculate tailoring the fair-haired Adonis's broad shoulders lifted and fell as if the matter was of little concern. 'And Natalie? Is that a name you inherited?'

'No. Actually, it was the name of my mum's best friend at school. She sadly died when she was a teenager and my mum called me Natalie as a tribute to her.'

'That was a nice gesture. If you don't mind my saying, there's something about you that suggests you are not wholly English…am I right?'

'I'm half-Greek. My mother was born and raised in Crete, although when she was seventeen she came to the UK to work.'

'What about your father?'

'He's English…from London.'

The enigmatic Ludo raised an amused sandy-coloured eyebrow. 'So you have the heat of the Mediterranean in your blood, along with the icy temperatures of the Thames? How intriguing.'

'That's certainly a novel way of putting it.' Struggling hard not to display her pique at the comment, and wondering at the same time how she could convey without offending him that she really craved some quiet time to herself before reaching London, Natalie frowned.

'I see I have offended you,' her enigmatic fellow passenger murmured, low-voiced. 'Forgive me. That was definitely not my intention.'

'Not at all. I just—I just have a lot of thinking to do before my meeting.'

'This meeting in London is work-related?'

Her lips briefly curved in a smile. 'I told you that my dad sent me the train ticket? Well, I'm going to meet him. I haven't seen him for about three months, and when we last spoke I sensed he was extremely worried about something... I just hope it's not his health. He's already suffered one heart attack as it is.' She shivered at the memory.

'I'm sorry. Does he live in the city?'

'Yes...he does.'

'But you live in Hampshire?'

'Yes...in a small village called Stillwater with my mum. Do you know it?'

'Indeed I do. I have a house that's about five miles from there in a place called Winter Lake.'

'Oh!' Winter Lake was known to be one of the most exclusive little enclaves in Hampshire. The locals referred to it as 'Billionaire's Row'. Natalie's initial assessment that Ludovic was a man of means had been spot-on, and she didn't know why but it made her feel strangely uneasy.

Leaning forward a little, he rested his hand on the arm of his seat and she briefly noticed the thick gold ring with an onyx setting he wore on his little finger. It might be some kind of family heirloom. But she was quickly distracted from the observation by his stunning sapphire gaze.

'I presume your parents must be divorced if you live with your mother?' he deduced.

'Yes, they are. In any case, tonight I'll be staying at my dad's place...we have a lot of catching up to do.'

'You are close...you and your father?'

The unexpected question took her aback. Staring into the fathomless, long-lashed blue eyes, for a long moment Natalie didn't know how to answer him. Or how much she might safely tell him.

'We definitely were when I was younger. After my parents divorced it was…well, it was very difficult for a while. It's got much better in the last couple of years, though. Anyway, he's the only dad I have, and I do care about him—which is why I'm anxious to get to London and find out what's been troubling him.'

'I can tell that you are a devoted and kind daughter. Your father is a very fortunate man indeed to have you worry about him.'

'I *endeavour* to be kind and devoted. Though, to be frank, there are times when it isn't easy. He can be rather unpredictable and not always easy to understand.' She couldn't help reddening at the confession. What on earth was she doing, admitting such a personal thing to a total stranger? To divert her anxiety she asked, 'Are you a father? I mean, do you have children?'

When she saw the wry quirk of his beautifully sculpted mouth she immediately regretted it, surmising that she'd transgressed some unspoken boundary.

'No. It is my view that children need a steady and stable environment, and right now my life is far too demanding and busy to provide that.'

'Presumably you'd have to be in a steady relationship too?'

Ludo's magnetically blue eyes flashed a little, as though he was amused, but Natalie guessed he was in no hurry to enlighten her as to his romantic status. Why should he be? After all, she was just some nondescript girl he had spontaneously assisted because she'd stupidly left her train ticket in the ladies' room before boarding the train.

'Indeed.'

His short reply was intriguingly enigmatic. Feeling suddenly awkward at the thought of engaging in further conversation, Natalie stifled a helpless yawn and immediately seized on it as the escape route she was subconsciously searching for.

'I think I'll close my eyes for a while, if you don't mind. I went out to dinner last night with a friend, to help celebrate her birthday, and didn't get in until late. The lack of sleep has suddenly caught up with me.'

'Go ahead. Try and get some rest. In any case I have some work to catch up on.' Ludo gestured towards the slim silver laptop that was open on the table in front of him. 'We will talk later.'

It sounded strangely like a promise.

With the memory of his smoky, arresting voice drifting tantalisingly through her mind like the most delicious warm breeze, Natalie leaned back in her luxurious seat, shut her eyes and promptly fell asleep...

In the generous landscaped garden of her childhood London home she squealed with excitement as her dad laughingly spun her round and round.

'Stop, Daddy, stop! You're making me dizzy!' she cried.

As she spun, she glimpsed tantalising snatches of blue summer sky, and the sun on her face filled her with such a sense of well-being that she could have hugged herself. In the background the air was suffused with the lilting chorus of enchanting birdsong. The idyll was

*briefly interrupted by her mother calling out to them
that tea was ready.*

The poignant dream ended as abruptly as it had
begun. Natalie felt distraught at not being able to sum-
mon it back immediately. When she was little, she'd
truly believed that life was wonderful. She'd felt safe
and secure and her parents had always seemed so happy
together.

A short while after the memory of her dream started
to fade, the muted sound of the doors opening stirred
her awake just in time to see a uniformed member of
staff enter the compartment with a refreshment trolley.
She was a young, slim woman, with neatly tied back
auburn hair and a cheery smile.

'Would you like something to eat or drink, sir?' She
addressed Ludo.

With a gently amused lift of his eyebrows, he turned
his head towards Natalie.

'I see that you have returned to the land of the living. Are you ready for some coffee and a sandwich?'
he asked. 'It's almost lunchtime.'

'Is it, really?' Feeling a little groggy, she straightened
in her seat and automatically checked her watch. She
was stunned to realise that she'd been asleep for almost
an hour. 'A cup of coffee would be great,' she said, digging into her purse for some change.

'Put your money away,' her companion ordered,
frowning. 'I will get this. How do you take your coffee? Black or white?'

'White with one sugar, please.'

'What about a sandwich?' He turned to the uniformed assistant, 'May I see a menu?' he asked.

When the girl handed a copy of said menu over to
him, he passed it straight to Natalie. About to tell him
that she wasn't hungry, she felt her stomach betray her
with an audible growl. Feeling her face flame red, she
glanced down at the list displayed in slim gold letter-
ing on the leaflet in front of her.

'I'll have a ham and Dijon mustard sandwich on
wholemeal bread, please. Thank you.'

'Make that two of those, and a black coffee along
with the white one.' He gave the assistant their order,
then waited until she'd arranged their drinks and sand-
wiches on the table and departed before speaking again.
'You sounded a little disturbed when you were dozing,'
he commented.

Natalie froze. Remembering her dream, and thinking
that she must have inadvertently cried out at the very
real sensation of her dad spinning her round and round,
she answered, 'Do you mean I was talking in my sleep?'

'No. You were, however, gently snoring,' he teased.

Now she really *did* wish the floor would open up
and swallow her. As the train powered through the lush
green countryside she hardly registered the sublime
views because she was so incensed.

'I don't snore. I've never snored in my life,' she re-
torted defensively. Seeing that Ludo was still smiling,
she added uncertainly, 'At least…not that I know of.'

'Your boyfriend is probably too polite to tell you.'
He grinned, taking a careful sip of his steaming black
coffee.

Her heart thudded hard at the implication. Not remotely amused, she stared fixedly back at the perfectly sculpted profile on the other side of the aisle. 'I don't have a boyfriend. And even if I had you shouldn't assume that we would—' Her impassioned little speech tailed off beneath the disturbing beam of Ludo's electric blue eyes.

'Sleep together?' he drawled softly.

Anxious not to come across as hopelessly inexperienced and naive to someone who was clearly an accomplished and polished man of the world and about as far out of her reach socially as the earth was from the planet Jupiter, Natalie bit into her sandwich and quickly stirred some sugar into her coffee.

'This is good,' she murmured. 'I didn't realise how hungry I was. But then I suppose it's because I didn't have any breakfast this morning.'

'You should always endeavour to eat breakfast.'

'That's what my mum says.'

'You told me earlier that she was from Crete?'

The less tricky question alleviated her previous embarrassment a little. Even though she had only visited the country a couple of times, she'd grown up on her mother's enchanting tales of her childhood homeland, and she would happily talk about Greece until the cows came home. 'That's right. Have you been there?'

'I have. It is a very beautiful island.'

'I've only been there a couple of times but I'd love to go again.' Her grey eyes shone. 'But somehow or other, time passes and work and other commitments inevitably get in the way.'

'You must have a demanding career?'

Natalie smiled. 'It's hardly a career, but I'm extremely glad that I chose it. My mum and I run a small but busy bed and breakfast together.'

'And what do you enjoy most about the enterprise? The day-to-day practicalities, such as greeting guests, making beds and cooking meals? Or do you perhaps like running the business side of things?'

Privately she confessed to being inspired to do what she did because her dad had run an extremely successful hotel business. As she'd grown older she'd picked up some useful tips from him along the way, in spite of the eventual dissolution of her parents' marriage.

'A bit of both, really,' she replied. 'But it's my mum that does most of the meeting and greeting. She's the most sublime hostess and cook, and the guests just adore her. Taking care of the business side of things and making sure that everything runs smoothly is my responsibility. I suppose it comes more naturally to me than to her.'

Ludo's compelling sapphire-coloured eyes crinkled at the corners. 'So...you like being in charge?'

The comment instigated an unsettling sensation of vague embarrassment. Did he perhaps think that she was boasting? 'Does that make me sound bossy and controlling?' she quizzed him.

Her handsome companion shook his head, 'Not at all. Why be defensive about an ability to take charge when a situation calls for it...especially in business? A going concern could hardly be successful if someone didn't take the reins. In my view it is a very admirable and desirable asset.'

'Thanks.' Even as she shyly acknowledged the unexpected compliment it suddenly dawned on Natalie that Ludo had revealed very little about himself. Yet he had somehow got her to divulge quite a lot about her own life.

Was he a psychologist, perhaps? Judging by his extremely confident manner and expensive clothing, whatever profession he was in it must earn him a fortune. She realised that she really *wanted* to know a bit more about him. What sentient woman wouldn't be interested in such a rivetingly attractive man? Maybe it was time she turned the tables and asked *him* some questions.

'Do you mind if I ask you what *you* do for a living?' she ventured.

Ludo blinked. Then he stared straight ahead of him for seemingly interminable seconds, before finally turning his head and gifting her with one of his magnetically compelling smiles. Her heart jumped as she found her glance irretrievably captured and taken hostage.

'My business is diverse. I have interests in many different things, Natalie.'

'So you run a business?'

He shrugged disconcertingly. Why was he being so cagey? Did he think she was hitting on him because he was wealthy? The very idea made her squirm—especially when he had displayed such rare kindness in paying for her train ticket. Not one in a thousand people would have been so generous towards a complete stranger, she was sure.

'I would rather not spoil this unexpectedly enjoyable train journey with you by discussing what I do,' he explained. 'Besides…I would much rather talk about you.'

'I've already told you what I do.'

'But what you do, Natalie, is not who you are. I would like to know a little bit more about your life…the things that interest you and why.'

She flushed. Such a bold and unexpected declaration briefly struck her dumb, and coupled with the admission that he was enjoying travelling with her, it made her feel strangely weak with pleasure. The last time she could recall feeling a similar pleasure was when she'd had her first kiss from a boy at school she'd had a massive crush on. Her interest in him hadn't lasted for more than a few months, but she'd never forgotten the tingle of fierce excitement the kiss had given her. It had been tender and innocently explorative, and she remembered it fondly.

Threading her fingers through her long, gently mussed hair, she lowered her gaze and immediately felt strangely bereft of Ludo's crystalline blue glance. What would a kiss from *his* lips feel like? It certainly wouldn't be like an inexperienced schoolboy's.

Disturbed by the thought, she drew in a steadying breath. 'If you mean my favourite pastimes or hobbies, I'm sure if I told you what they were you'd think them quite ordinary and boring.'

'Try me,' he invited with a smile.

Natalie almost said out loud, *When you look at me like that I can't think of a single thing I like except the dimples in your carved cheekbones when you smile.*

Shocked by the intensity of heat that washed through her at the private admission, she briefly glanced away to compose herself. 'I enjoy simple pleasures, like reading and going to the cinema. I just love watching a good film that takes me away from the worries and concerns of my own life and transports me into the story of someone else's…especially if it's uplifting. I also love listening to music and taking long walks in the countryside or on the beach.'

'I find none of those interests either boring or ordinary,' Ludo replied, the edges of his finely sculpted lips nudging the wryest of smiles. 'Besides, sometimes the most ordinary things in life—the things we may take for granted—can be the best. Don't you agree? I only wish I had more time to enjoy some of the pleasures that you mention myself.'

'Why can't you free up some time so that you can? Do you have to be so busy *all* of the time?'

Frowning deeply, he seemed to consider the question for an unsettlingly long time. His perusal of Natalie while he was mulling over her question bordered on intense. Flustered, she averted her gaze to check the time on her watch.

'We'll soon be arriving in London,' she announced, reaching over to the window seat for her bag and delving into it for a pen and something to write on. 'Do you think you could give me your full name and address now, so I can send you the money for my ticket?'

'We might as well wait until we disembark.'

He bit into his sandwich, as if certain she wouldn't give him an argument. She wanted to insist, but in the end decided not to. What difference could it possibly make to take his address now or later, as long as she got it? 'Never a borrower or a lender be,' her mother had always told her. 'And always pay your debts.'

Instead of adding any further comment, Natalie fell into a reflective silence. Observing that she wasn't eating her lunch, Ludo frowned, and the gesture brought two deep furrows to his otherwise silkily smooth brow.

'Finish your food,' he advised. 'If you haven't had any breakfast you'll need it. Especially if you face a difficult meeting with your father.'

'Difficult?'

'I mean emotional. If his health has deteriorated then your discussion will not be easy for either of you.'

The comment made a jolt of fear scissor through her heart. She was genuinely afraid that her dad's urgent need to see her was to tell her he'd received a serious diagnosis from the doctor. They'd had their ups and downs over the years but she still adored him, and would hate for him to be taken from her when he had only just turned sixty.

'You're right. No doubt it will be emotional.' She gave him a self-conscious smile and chewed thoughtfully on her sandwich.

'I'm sure that whatever happens the two of you will find great reassurance in each other's company.'

The sudden ring of Ludo's mobile instantly commanded his attention. After a brief acknowledgement to the caller, he covered the speaker with his hand and turned back to Natalie.

'I'm afraid I need to take this call. I'm going to step outside into the corridor for a few minutes.'

As he rose to his feet she was taken aback to see how tall he was…at least six foot two, she mused. The impressive physique beneath the flawless Italian tailoring hinted at an athletically lean and muscular build, and she couldn't help staring up at him in admiration. Concerned that she might resemble a besotted teenager, staring open-mouthed at a pop idol, she forced herself to relax and nod her head in acknowledgement.

'Please, go ahead.'

As the automatic twin doors of the compartment swished open Ludo turned to her for a moment and, with a disconcerting twinkle in his eye, said, 'Whatever you do, don't run away, Natalie…will you?'

CHAPTER TWO

'I ASSUME THAT all the papers are ready?'

Even as he asked the question Ludo rapidly assessed the detailed information he'd been given, turning it over in his mind with the usual rapier-like thoroughness that enabled him to dive into every corner and crevice of a situation all at once and miss nothing.

At the other end of the line, his personal assistant Nick confirmed that everything was as it should be. Rubbing a hand round his clean-shaven, chiselled jaw, Ludo enquired 'And you've scheduled the meeting for tomorrow, as I asked?'

'Yes, I have. I told the client that he and his lawyer should come to the office at ten forty-five, just as you instructed.'

'And you've obviously notified Godrich, my own man?'

'Of course.'

'Good. It sounds like you've taken care of everything. I'll see you back at the office some time this afternoon to give the papers a final once-over. Bye for now.'

When he'd concluded the call Ludo leant his back against the panelled wall of the train corridor, trying in vain to calm the uncharacteristic nerves that were fluttering like a swarm of intoxicated butterflies in the pit of his stomach. It wasn't the call or its contents that had perturbed him. Finalising deals and acquiring potentially lucrative businesses that had fallen on hard times was meat and drink to him, and he was famed for quickly turning his new acquisitions into veins of easily flowing gold. It was how he had made his fortune.

No, the reason for his current disquiet was his engaging fellow passenger. How could a mere slip of a girl, with the reed-slim figure of a prima ballerina, long brown hair and big grey eyes like twin sunlit pools, electrify him as if he'd been plugged into the National Grid?

He shook his head. She wasn't anything like the voluptuous blondes and redheads that he was usually attracted to, and yet there was something irresistibly engaging about her. In fact, from the moment Ludo had heard the sound of her soft voice she had all but seduced him… Even more surprising than that, what were the odds that she should turn out to be half-Greek? The synchronicity stunned him.

Distractedly staring down at several missed messages on his phone, he impatiently flicked off the screen and gazed out of the window at the scenery that was hurtling by instead. The mixture of old and new industrial buildings and the now familiar twenty-first-century constructions rising high into the skyline heralded the fact that they were fast approaching the city. It was time he made up his mind about whether or not he wanted to act on the intense attraction that had gripped him and decide what to do about it. It was clear that the

lovely Natalie was in earnest about reimbursing him
for her train ticket, but he was naturally wary of giving his home address to strangers…however charming
and pretty.

Although she'd transfixed him from the moment
she'd stepped breathlessly into the first-class compartment and he'd scented the subtle but arresting tones of
her mandarin and rose perfume, it wasn't in his nature
to make snap decisions. While he was a great believer in
following strong impulses in his business life, he wasn't
so quick to apply the same method to his romantic liai-
sons. Sexual desire could be dangerously misleading,
he'd found. It might be tempting as far as satisfying his
healthy libido, but not if it turned into a headache he
could well do without.

Sadly, he'd had a few of those in his time. He didn't
mind treating his dates to beautiful *haute couture* clothing or exquisite jewellery from time to time, but Ludo
had discovered to his cost that the fairer sex always
wanted so much more than he was willing to give. More
often than not, top of the list of what they wanted was a
proposal of marriage. Even his vast wealth couldn't cush-
ion him from the disagreeable inevitability of another
broken relationship because the woman concerned had
developed certain expectations of him…expectations
that he definitely wasn't ready to fulfil. No matter *how*
much his beloved family reminded him that it was about
time he settled down with someone.

His mother's greatest desire was to become a grand-
mother. At thirty-six, and her only son, Ludo seemed
to be constantly disappointing her because he wasn't

any closer to fulfilling her wish. She was desperate for him to meet a suitable girl—'suitable' meaning someone who she and his father approved of. But it wasn't easy to meet genuinely caring and loving women who desired a relationship and children more than wealth and position, he'd found. And when his wealth and reputation preceded him it was apt to attract the very kind of shallow, ambitious women he should avoid.

Frankly, Ludo was heartily tired of that particular unhappy merry-go-round. The truth was, in his heart he yearned to find a soulmate—if such a creature even existed—someone warm and intelligent, with a good sense of humour and a genuinely kind disposition. He returned his thoughts to Natalie. If he embarked on a relationship with her and she should learn that he was as rich as a modern-day Croesus and counted some of the most influential business people in Europe as his friends, then he would never be sure that she was dating him for himself and *not* his money. Already he'd inadvertently let slip that he lived in the affluent area of Winter Lake. But then she must surely guess he wasn't short of money if he was travelling first class and could spontaneously pay for her ticket?

Regarding the ticket she'd lost, she'd told him that her father had sent it to her. Was *he* a wealthy man? Surely he must be. If that was the case then the pretty Natalie must have been used to a certain level of comfort before her parents had divorced. Would she be holding out for someone equally wealthy—if not more so—in a relationship?

Frowning, Ludo quickly decided it would make sense

to ask for her phone number if he wanted to see her again, rather than give her his address. That way *he* would be the one in control of the situation, and if he should glean at any time that she was a gold-digger then he would drop her like a hot potato. Meanwhile, they could meet up for a drink while she was in London under the perfectly legitimate excuse of his allowing her to settle her debt. If after that things progressed satisfactorily between them, then Ludo would be only too happy to supply more personal information, such as his full address.

Feeling satisfied with his decision, he exhaled a sigh, briefly tunnelled his fingers through his floppily perfect hair, and slipped his mobile into the silk-lined pocket of his jacket. Before depressing the button that opened the automatic doors into the first-class compartment he stole a surreptitious glance through the glass at the slender, doe-eyed brunette who was gazing out of the window with her chin in her hand, as if daydreaming. His lips automatically curved into a smile. He couldn't help anticipating her willing agreement to meet up with him for a date. What reason could she possibly have *not* to?

'I don't understand. You're saying you want to meet me for a drink?'

Blinking in disbelief at the imposing Adonis who was surveying her with a wry twist of his carved lips as they stood together on the busy station platform, Natalie convinced herself she must have become hard of hearing. Ludo's surprising suggestion sounded very much as if he was inviting her out on a date. But why on earth would he do such a thing? It just didn't make sense. Perhaps she'd simply got the wrong end of the stick.

Practically every other woman who'd disembarked from the train was stealing covetous glances over her shoulder at the handsome and stylishly dressed man standing in front of her as she hurried by, she noticed. No doubt they were privately wondering why a girl as unremarkable as herself should capture his attention for so much as a second. Her heart skipped one or two anxious beats.

'Yes, I do,' he replied.

His jaw firmed and his blue eyes shimmered enigmatically. For Natalie, meeting such an arresting glance was like standing in the eye of a sultry tropical storm—it shook her as the wind shook a fragile sapling, threatening to uproot it. She held her voluminous red leather bag over her chest, as though it were some kind of protective shield, and couldn't help frowning. Instead of sending her self-esteem soaring, Ludo's suggestion that they meet up for a drink had had the opposite effect on her confidence. It hardly helped that in faded jeans and a floral print gypsy-style blouse she felt singularly dowdy next to him in his expensive Italian tailoring.

'Why?' she asked. 'I only asked for your address so that I can send you the money for my train fare. You've already indicated that you're a very busy man, so why would you go to all the trouble of meeting up with me instead of simply letting me post you a cheque?'

Her companion shook his head bemusedly, as if he couldn't fathom what must be, to him, a very untypical response. Natalie guessed he wasn't used to women turning him down for anything.

'Aside from allowing you to personally pay me back for the ticket, I'd like to see you again, Natalie,' he stated seriously. 'Did such a possibility not occur to you? After all, you indicated to me on the train that you were a free agent…remember?'

Unfortunately, she had. She'd confessed she didn't have a boyfriend when Ludo had assumed that if she had he must be too polite to tell her that she snored in her sleep. She blushed so hard at the memory that her delicate skin felt as if she stood bare inches from a roaring fire.

Adjusting her bag, she endeavoured to meet the steady, unwavering gaze that was so uncomfortably searing her. 'Are *you* a free agent?' she challenged. 'For all I know you could be married with six children.'

He tipped back his head and released a short, heart-felt laugh. Never before had the sound of a man's amusement brushed so sensually over her nerve-endings—as though he had stroked down her bare skin with the softest, most delicate feather. Out of the blue, a powerful ache to see him again infiltrated her blood and wouldn't be ignored…even if he *did* inhabit an entirely different stratosphere from her.

'I can assure you that I am neither married nor the father of six children. I told you before that I've been far too busy for that. Don't you believe me?'

Ludo's expression had become serious once more. Conscious of the now diminishing crowd leaving the train, and realising with relief that they were no longer the focus of unwanted interest, Natalie shrugged.

'All I'll say is that I hope you're telling me the truth. Honesty is really important to me. All right, then. When do you want us to meet?'

'How long do you think you'll be in London?'

'Probably a couple of days at most…that is unless my dad needs me around for longer.' Once again she was unable to control the tremor of fear in her voice at the thought that her father might be seriously ill. To stop from dwelling on the subject, and to prevent any un-comfortable quizzing from Ludo, she smiled and added quickly, 'I'll just have to wait and see, won't I?'

'If you are only going to be staying in town for a cou-ple of days, that doesn't give us very much time. That being the case, I think we should meet up tomorrow evening, don't you?' There was an unexpected glint of satisfied expectation in his eyes. 'I can book us a table at Claridges. What time would suit you best?'

'The restaurant, you mean? I thought you said we were only meeting for a drink?'

'Don't you eat in the evenings?'

'Of course, but—'

'What time?'

'Eight o'clock?'

'Eight o'clock it is, then. Let me have your mobile number so I can ring you if I'm going to be delayed.'

Her brow puckering, Natalie was thoughtful. 'Okay, I'll give it to you. But don't forget it might be me who's delayed or can't make it if my dad isn't well…in which case you'd better let me have *your* number.'

With another one of his enigmatic smiles, Ludo acquiesced unhesitatingly.

She'd never got used to a doorman letting her into the rather grand Victorian building where her father's luxurious flat was situated. It made her feel like an audacious usurper pretending to be someone important.

The contrast between how her parents lived was like night and day. Her mother was a conscientious and devoted home-maker who enjoyed the simple and natural things in life, while her father was a real hedonist who loved material things perhaps a little *too* much. Although undoubtedly hard-working, he had a tendency to be quite reckless with his money.

Now, as she found herself travelling up to the topmost floor in the lift, Natalie refused to dwell on that. Instead she found herself growing more and more uneasy at what he might be going to tell her.

When Bill Carr opened the door to greet her, straight away his appearance seemed to confirm her worst suspicions. She was shocked at how much he'd aged since she'd last seen him. It had only been three months, but the change in him was so marked it might as well have been three years. He was a tall, handsome, distinguished-looking man, with a penchant for traditionally tailored Savile Row suits, and his still abundant silvergrey hair was always impeccably cut and styled...*but not today.* Today it was messy and in dire need of attention. His white shirt was crumpled and unironed and his pinstriped trousers looked as if he'd slept in them.

With alarm Natalie noticed that he carried a crystal

tumbler that appeared to have a generous amount of whisky in it. The reek of alcohol when he opened his mouth to greet her confirmed it.

'Natalie! Thank God you're here, sweetheart. I was going out of my mind, thinking that you weren't going to come.'

He flung an arm round her and pulled her head down onto his chest. Natalie dropped her bag to the ground and did her utmost to relax. Instinct told her that whatever had made her father seek solace in strong drink must be more serious than she'd thought.

Lifting her head she endeavoured to make her smile reassuring. 'I'd never have let you down, Dad.' Reaching up, she planted an affectionate kiss on his unshaven cheek as the faintest whiff of his favourite aftershave mingled with the incongruous and far less appealing smell of whisky.

'Did you have a good journey?' he asked, reaching over her shoulder to push the door shut behind her.

'I did, thanks. It was really nice to travel first class, but you shouldn't have gone to such unnecessary expense, Dad.'

Even as she spoke Natalie couldn't help but recall her meeting with Ludo, and the fact that he'd stumped up the money for her ticket when he'd heard her explain to the guard that she'd lost hers. His name was short for Ludovic, he'd told her. For a few seconds she lost herself in a helpless delicious reverie. The name was perfect. She really liked it…*she liked it a lot*. There was an air of mystery about the sound of it…a bit like its owner. They hadn't exchanged surnames but every second of their time together on the train was indelibly imprinted on her mind, never to be forgotten. Particularly his cultured, sexy voice and those extraordinarily beautiful sapphire-blue eyes of his. Her heart jumped when she nervously recalled her agreement to meet him for dinner tomorrow...

'I've always wanted to give you the best of everything, sweetheart...and that didn't change when your mother and I split up. Is she well, by the way?'

Her father's curiously intense expression catapulted her back to the present, and Natalie saw the pain that he still carried over the break-up with his wife. Her mouth dried uncomfortably as she privately empathised with the loss that clearly still haunted him.

'Yes, she's very well. She asked me to tell you that she hopes you're doing well too.'

He grimaced and shrugged. 'She's a good woman, your mother. The best woman I ever knew. It's a crying shame I didn't appreciate her more when we were together. As to your comment that she hopes I'm doing well... It near kills me to have to admit this, darling, but I'm afraid I'm not doing very well at all. Come into the kitchen and let me get you a cup of tea, then I'll explain what's been going on.'

The admission confirmed her increasingly anxious suspicions, but it still tore at Natalie's insides to hear him say it. Feeling suddenly drained, she followed his tall, rangy frame into his modern stainless-steel kitchen, watched him accidentally splash water over his crumpled sleeve as he filled the kettle at the tap—was she imagining it, or was his hand shaking a little?—and plugged it into the wall socket. He collected his whisky glass before dropping wearily down onto a nearby stool.

'What is it, Dad? Have you been having pains in your chest again? Is that why you wanted to see me so urgently? Please tell me.'

Her father imbibed a generous slug of whisky, then slammed his glass noisily back down on the counter, rubbing the back of his hand across his eyes. Communication was suspended for several disturbing moments as he looked to be struggling to gather his thoughts. 'For once it's not my health that's at stake, here, Nat. It's my livelihood.' His mouth shaped a rueful grimace.

Outside, from the busy street below, came the jarring sound of a car horn honking. Natalie flinched in shock. Drawing in a steadying breath, she saw that her dad was perfectly serious in his confession.

'Has something gone wrong with the business? Is it to do with a downturn in profits? I know the country's going through a tough time economically at the moment, but you can weather the storm, Dad…you always do.'

Bill Carr looked grim. 'The hotel chain hasn't made any profit for nearly two years, my love…largely because I haven't kept up with essential refurbishment and modernisation. And I can no longer afford to keep on staff of the calibre that helped make it such a success in the first place. It's so like you to blame it on the economy, but that just isn't the case.'

'Then if it's not that *why* can't you afford to modernise or keep good staff? You've always told me that the business has made you a fortune.'

'That's perfectly true. It *did* make a fortune. But

sadly I haven't been able to hold on to it. I've lost almost everything, Natalie…and I'm afraid I'm being forced to sell the business at a loss to try and recoup some money and pay off the vast amount of debt I've accrued.'

Natalie's insides lurched as though she'd just narrowly escaped plunging down a disused elevator shaft. 'It's really that bad?' she murmured, hardly knowing what to say.

Her father pushed to his feet, despondently shaking his head. 'I've made such a mess of my life,' he told her, 'and I suppose because I've been so reckless and irresponsible the chickens have come home to roost, as they say. I deserve it. I was blessed with everything a man could wish for—a beautiful wife, a lovely daughter and work that I loved… But I threw it all away because I became more interested in seeking pleasure than keeping a proper eye on the business.'

'You mean women and drink?'

'And the rest. It's not hard to understand why I had a heart attack.'

Needing to offer him some comfort and reassurance, even though she was shocked and slightly dazed at what 'the rest' might refer to, Natalie urgently caught hold of his hand and folded it between her own.

'That doesn't mean you're going to have another one, Dad. Things will get better, I promise you. First of all, you've got to stop blaming yourself for what you did in the past and forgive yourself. Then you have to vow that you won't hurt yourself in that way ever again— that you'll look after yourself, move on, and deal with what's going on right now. You said you're being forced to sell the business at a loss…to whom?'

'A man who's known in the world of mergers and acquisitions as "the Alchemist" because he can turn dirt into diamonds at the drop of a hat it seems. A Greek billionaire named Petrakis. It's a cliché, I know, but he really did make me an offer I couldn't refuse. At least I know he's got the money. That's something, I suppose. The thing is I need cash in the bank as soon as possible, Nat. The bank wants the money from the sale in my account tomorrow, after we complete, or else they'll make me bankrupt.'

'Don't you have any other assets? What about this flat? Presumably you own it outright?'

Again her father shook his head. 'Mortgaged up to the hilt, I'm afraid.' Noting the shock in her eyes, he freed his hand from hers, winced, and started to rub his chest.

Natalie's own heart started to race with concern. 'Are you all right, Dad? Should I call a doctor?'

'I'm fine. I probably just need to rest a bit and stop drinking so much whisky. Perhaps you'd make me a cup of tea instead?'

'Of course I will. Why don't you go and put your feet up on the couch in the living room and I'll bring it in to you?'

His answer to her suggestion was to impel her close into his chest and plant a fond kiss on the top of her head. When she glanced up to examine his suddenly pale features, his warm smile was unstintingly loving and proud.

'You're a good girl, Natalie...the best daughter in the world. I regret not telling you that more often.'

'You and Mum might have parted, but I always knew that you loved me.' Gently, she stepped out of the circle of his arms.

'It does my heart good to hear you say that. I don't want to take advantage, but perhaps you won't mind me asking another favour of you?'

Her throat thick with emotion, Natalie smiled back at him. 'Ask away. You know that I'll do anything I can to help.'

'I want you to come with me to this meeting I've got with Petrakis and his lawyers tomorrow. Just for a little moral support. Will you?'

Instinctively she knew it would probably be one of the hardest things she'd ever done, watching her father sign away the business he'd worked so hard to build all these years to some fat-cat Greek billionaire who didn't have a clue about how much it meant to him, or care that the sale might be breaking his heart...

'Of course I will.' She lightly touched her palm to his cheek. 'Now, go and put your feet up, like I said. I'll make that cup of tea and bring it in to you.'

Her father's once broad shoulders were stooped as he turned to exit the room. Natalie had never felt remotely violent towards anyone before, but she did now as she thought of the Greek billionaire known as 'the Alchemist' who was buying his business from him for a song when he could no doubt well afford to purchase it for far more and at least give her dad a fighting chance to get back on his feet again...

CHAPTER THREE

IF NATALIE HAD had a restless night, then her father had
had a worse one. Several times she'd heard him get up
to pace the hallway outside their bedrooms, and once
when he'd omitted to close his door she'd heard the
sound of violent retching coming from his bathroom.
It had so frightened her that she'd raced straight into
his room and banged urgently on the en-suite door. He
had pleaded with her to let him sort himself out, telling her that it had happened before, that he knew how
to deal with it, and Natalie had reluctantly returned to
her room, heavy of heart and scared out of her wits in
case he should have a seizure or a fit during the night.

After not much more than three hours' sleep she'd
woken bleary-eyed and exhausted to find blinding sunshine beaming straight at her through the uncovered
window, where she'd forgotten to roll down the blinds.

After checking that her dad was awake, she stumbled into the kitchen to make a large pot of strong black
coffee. She rustled up some toast and marmalade and
called out to him to come to the table.

The dazzlingly bright sunshine wasn't exactly a good
friend to Bill Carr that morning, Natalie observed anx-

iously. The complexion that she'd judged as a little pasty yesterday looked ashen grey and sickly today. He made a feeble attempt at eating the toast she'd made, but didn't hesitate to down two large mugs of coffee.

Afterwards, he wiped the back of his trembling hand across his mouth, grimaced and said, 'I suppose you could say I'm ready for anything now.'

The weak smile he added to that statement all but broke Natalie's heart.

'You won't have to face this alone, Dad. I'll be with you every step of the way…I promise.'

'I know, darling. And, whilst I know I hardly deserve to have your support at all, I honestly appreciate it and one day soon I'll make it up to you…that's *my* promise to you.'

'You don't need to make it up to me. We're family, remember? All I want is for you to be well and happy. Now, remind me what time we have to be at this Petrakis's office?'

'Ten forty-five.'

'Okay. After I shower and dress I'll phone a cab to pick us up. Where is the office we're going to?'

'Westminster.'

'Not far away, then. Well, you'd better go and get ready, too. Do you need anything ironed?'

Getting to his feet and digging his hands deep into the capacious pockets of his dressing gown, her father seemed completely nonplussed by the question.

Taking in a consciously deep breath to calm her disquiet, Natalie asked, 'Do you want me to come with you and check?'

'No, darling, it's fine. I'm wearing my best Savile Row suit, and my one ironed shirt has been hanging in the wardrobe ready ever since I got the call that the meeting was today.'

'Good.' Giving him an approving smile, Natalie stole a brief glance at the fashionably utilitarian stainless-steel clock on the wall. 'We'd better get our skates on, then. We don't want to be late.'

'For the execution, you mean?' His grimace, clearly tinged with bitterness and regret, had never looked more pained. Yet the comment also contained a hint of ironic humour.

'I know it must be hard for you to contemplate letting go of the business that you put your heart and soul into to building,' she sympathised, 'but maybe this could be an exciting new start for you. An opportunity to put your energies into something else…something a little less taxing that you could manage more easily. Even the direst situations can have a silver lining.'

'And how am I going to start another business if I have barely a penny to my name?'

'Is running a business the only way you can earn a living?'

'That's all I know how to do.' Exhaling a leaden sigh, her father drove his fingers exasperatedly through his already mussed silver hair.

Struggling with her personal sense of frustration at not being able to find an instant solution that would cheer him and give him some hope, Natalie dropped her hands to hips clad in the pyjama bottoms and T-shirt she'd borrowed from him to wear to bed and thought hard.

'What if we ask this Petrakis if he could extend some humanitarian understanding and pay you a reasonable sum for the business? After all, if you say he has a reputation for being able to turn dirt into diamonds then surely he must know that he's bound to make another fortune from your hotel chain? What would it hurt for him to pay you a fairer price?'

'Sweetheart...I don't mean this unkindly, but you know very little about men like Petrakis. How do you think he acquired his considerable fortune? It wasn't from taking a humanitarian approach to making money! Whatever you say to him, however impassioned or eloquent your argument, it would be like water off a duck's back.'

Natalie's grey eyes flashed angrily. 'And that's how the business world measures success these days, is it? Someone is only thought of as successful if he's single-mindedly ruthless in his dealings and doesn't give a fig about the psychological damage he might cause to anyone—not even a fellow entrepreneur who's down on his luck—just as long as he can get what he wants?'

Breathing hard, she knew how much she already despised the Greek billionaire even though she hadn't even set eyes on him yet. But there was also something else on her mind. If this meeting with Petrakis was too devastating for her dad—and she'd certainly be able to tell if it was—then she couldn't abandon him later on tonight to go and have dinner with the enigmatic Ludo. Even though she'd barely been able to cease thinking about the man since meeting him on the train yesterday...

'Apparently that is the case. But don't distress yourself by being angry on my behalf, love. I know I asked you to come with me for moral support, but this isn't your battle. It's mine. Now, I think we'd better go and get ourselves ready.'

Giving a resigned shrug, her father turned on his heel. With a heavy tread he made his way down the varnished wood-panelled hall to his bedroom, as if carrying the weight of the world on his shoulders.

'Ludovic...how are you? Traffic's bloody awful out there today. Everything's moving at a snail's pace.'

Ludo had been staring out of the window of his plush Westminster office, hardly registering anything on the road outside because his mind was fixed on one thought and one thought only. Tonight he was meeting the exquisite Natalie for dinner. He closed his eyes. For just a few short seconds he could imagine himself becoming entranced by the still, crystal-clear lake of her gaze all over again, and could conjure up the alluring scent of her perfume as easily as if she were standing right next to him. It was impossible to recall the last time he'd had this sense of excited anticipation fluttering in the pit of his stomach at the prospect of seeing a woman again...if it had *ever* happened at all. So, when the booming voice of his public-school-educated lawyer Stephen Godrich unexpectedly rang out behind him he was so immersed in his daydream that he almost jumped out of his skin.

With a wry smile he pivoted, immediately steering

his mind back into work mode. There would be time for more fantasies about the lovely Natalie later, after they'd met for dinner, Ludo was sure.

Automatically stepping forward to shake the other man's hand, he privately noted that the buttons on the bespoke suit jacket he wore had about as much hope of meeting over his ever-expanding girth as Ludo had of winning the Men's Final at Wimbledon... An impossibility, of course, seeing as polo was his sport of choice, and not tennis.

'Hello, Stephen. You're looking well...in fact so well I fear I must be paying you too much,' he joked.

The other man's pebble-sized blue eyes, almost consumed by the generous flesh that surrounded them, flickered with momentary alarm. Quickly recovering, he drew out a large checked handkerchief from his trouser pocket and proceeded to mop the perspiration that glazed his brow.

'Being an inveterate lover of fine dining definitely has its price, my friend,' he remarked, smiling. 'I know I should be more self-disciplined, but we all have our little peccadillos, don't we? Anyway...do you mind if I ask if your client has arrived yet?'

Glancing down at the platinum Rolex that encircled his tanned wrist, Ludo frowned. 'I'm afraid not. It looks like he may well be late. While we're waiting for him I'll get Jane to make us some coffee.'

'Splendid idea. A few choice biscuits wouldn't go amiss either, if you have some,' the lawyer added hopefully.

Already at the door on his way out to Reception,

Ludo raised a hand in acknowledgement, thinking that if the man would only cut down on his sugar intake his handmade suits might fit him a whole lot better.

Ludo and his trusted representative Amelia Redmond—who had put the bid in for the once prestigious hotel chain on his behalf—sat at the polished table in the boardroom along with Stephen Godrich and Ludo's affable and highly professional assistant Nick. The younger man was re-reading some documentation in front of him and his olive-skinned brow was furrowed in concentration. Why it should suddenly occur to him at that precise moment that Nick's family came from Crete, he didn't know. Except that he'd been thinking about Natalie again, and he recalled her telling him that her mother had grown up there.

Suddenly impatient to have this meeting over and done with—even though the purchase of this particular hospitality business was a genuine coup—he had a strong urge to take some time out from work to go for a swim at his private health club. Not for the first time he recalled the surprising question Natalie had posed to him on the train. 'Do you have to be so busy *all* of the time?' she'd asked.

Ludo frowned. His family had raised him with a bulldog work ethic second to none, and he'd more than reaped the rewards of his tenacity and hard work. Yet there was still a perverse sense of not being deserving enough running through his veins that didn't always allow him to enjoy those rewards. Somewhere along the line he'd forgotten that a body needed rest and relaxation from time to time to recharge its batteries. Lord knew he could easily afford to take a year off or more if he wanted to. But to do what? And, more to the point, with *whom*?

Straightening the cuffs of his pristine cobalt shirt, he glanced up, intuiting the entrance of his diminutive middle-aged secretary Jane a moment before she appeared in the doorway.

'Mr Carr is here, along with his daughter and his solicitor Mr Nichols,' she announced gravely, as was her habit. 'Shall I show them in?'

'Please do. Have you asked them what refreshments they'd like?'

'I have.'

At the back of his mind Ludo was wondering why Bill Carr had brought his daughter along to the meeting. Neither Nick nor the ultra-efficient Amelia Redmond had informed him that she had any shares in the business, and the last thing he wanted to deal with today was some unforeseen complication that affected the deal. The look on Nick's face told him that he was equally puzzled by the daughter's attendance. As Jane held the door wide, so that the trio in reception could enter, Ludo was the first to rise to his feet to greet them.

When he registered that the pretty brunette who came in with the two men was Natalie he honestly thought his heart was going to jump clear out of his chest.

He stared. Natalie was the *daughter* of the hotel chain's owner, Bill Carr? Was fate playing some kind of outlandish joke on him? The wide-eyed liquid-silver glance that mirrored his own profound sense of shock instantly had him hypnotised, and he couldn't help but murmur her name beneath his breath. It was impossible to deny the instantaneous jolt of almost violent attraction that zigzagged through him at seeing her again.

The faded jeans that hugged her long slim legs and the cerise satin tunic she wore were in direct contrast to everyone else's ultra formal attire. Yet he couldn't help thinking that the ensemble was utterly charming and refreshing. But, as much as he was secretly delighted to see her, Ludo knew potentially that this was one of the worst situations he could have wished for. Already he could sense that she was on her guard, but not by so much as a flicker of an eyelid did she indicate that she'd met him before. Clearly it was going to be hard for her to trust him after realising that *he* was the man about to buy her father's business—and not at the best price either. She must know he was selling it at a substantial loss to Ludo.

Steering his glance deliberately over to the two men, in a bid to buy more time and think what to do, he asked, 'Which one of you is Bill Carr?'

He couldn't help his tone sounding on edge. In truth, Natalie's unexpected appearance, plus the astonishing fact that her father should turn out to be the businessman whose hotel chain he was purchasing, had seriously shaken him. As Ludo endeavoured to win back his equilibrium, the rangy, almost gaunt-looking man in a traditional grey pinstriped suit stepped forward to shake his hand.

'I am. This is my solicitor, Edward Nichols, and my daughter Natalie.'

Sadly, she *didn't* step forward to shake Ludo's hand.

Instead, her beautiful grey eyes flashed a warning, as if to tell him that under the circumstances it would be unwise to acknowledge her personally. At that moment, he couldn't help but agree.

'I presume you must be Mr Petrakis?' Bill Carr finished.

'That's right,' Ludo responded, adding quickly, 'Why don't we all sit down? I understand that my secretary is seeing to some refreshments, but in the meantime allow me to introduce you to my colleagues.'

The introductions over, he reached for the glass of water on the leather blotter in front of him and took a cooling sip. Somehow he had to endeavour to compose himself and not let anyone see that the sight of Natalie had almost robbed him of the power of speech—never mind his ability to present himself with his usually inimitable self-assurance. After Jane had brought coffee and biscuits, then shut the door behind her, Ludo seized the opportunity to hand over the formalities of the deal to Amelia and Nick. While they outlined the offer he had proposed, Bill Carr and his solicitor listened intently, every so often asking questions and jotting down notes.

Due to the uncharacteristic guilt that assailed him because he was buying her father's business, the back of Ludo's neck prickled uncomfortably every time he inadvertently caught Natalie's eye.

He tried hard to recall everything she'd told him about the man when they'd spoken on the train yesterday. *'He can be rather unpredictable and not always easy to understand,'* she'd confided. Ludo wondered if that had anything to do with what he chose to spend his money on. His assistant Nick had uncovered a story in the business community about the man having a reputation for being reckless with his money. The story went that he regularly indulged in various costly habits…not all of them entirely wholesome. No doubt that was why he found himself in the painful position he was in now, having to sell his business for less than half its value to meet the debt those expensive habits had incurred…

Ludo's two assistants brought their outlining of the deal to a concise and professional conclusion. Then his solicitor confirmed the conditions of the sum being offered, to make sure that Bill Carr was fully aware of every aspect of the deal. All that remained after that was for the deal to be signed and witnessed and the money transferred to his bank account.

As Ludo's solicitor Stephen Godrich pushed the necessary document across the table for the man's signature, Natalie stopped them all in their tracks with a stunning question. 'Mr Petrakis…do you think that the amount you're offering my father for his business is entirely fair?'

Mr Petrakis? Ludo almost smiled at her deliberate formality. But immediately after his initial amused reaction he registered the less than flattering implication behind the soft-voiced enquiry.

'Fair?' He frowned, turning the full force of his sapphire-blue gaze on her lightly flushed face.

'Yes—fair. You must know that you're getting what is one of the most innovative and successful hotel chains in the UK for practically peanuts! You're a very wealthy man, I hear. Surely you can afford to pay a less insulting amount to a man whose ingenuity and hard work created the business in the first place, so he might invest some of it in another entrepreneurial venture and make his living?'

As Natalie's little speech came to an end it was as though a bomb had exploded. As if in fear of igniting another, no one moved a muscle or so much as rustled a piece of paper. They were all in shock.

Going by her pink cheeks and over-bright eyes, so was Natalie. As for himself, for a heart-pounding few moments Ludo was genuinely at a loss as to know how to answer. But then his well-honed instinct for self-preservation thankfully kicked in, along with the first stirrings of genuine fury.

Leaning towards her across the table, he linked his hands together to anchor himself. 'You consider what I am paying your father for his business *insulting,* do you?'

'Yes, I do.'

'Have you asked him how many other people put in tenders for it? If not, why don't you do that now? Go on—ask him.'

The man sitting next to her slid a long, bony-fingered hand across his daughter's.

'I know you mean well, love, but the fact is no one other than Mr Petrakis is interested in buying the hotel chain. No doubt he is a realist about making money in business—as *I* am. The current market is in a slump, and I'm actually grateful that someone has made me an offer. The hotel chain isn't the roaring success it once was, Natalie. Whoever buys it is going to have to invest a substantial amount of money to bring it up to scratch again and make it profitable. Maybe that's the point you need to realise.'

Natalie bit her lip, and her answering glance up at him was verging on sorrowful. 'But this whole thing has so badly affected your health, Dad. You know it has. What are you going to do for a living if you can't get another business venture off the ground? That's the only reason I want more money for you.'

Hearing the devotion and concern in her voice, Ludo couldn't help admiring her—even though her unbelievable accusation had temporarily embarrassed him. It wasn't hard to see that Natalie Carr was a naturally caring woman who clearly adored her father and quickly forgave him for any poor decisions or mistakes he'd made—even if those poor decisions and mistakes hurt *her*. All in all, it made the idea of a liaison with her even more attractive, and Ludo wasn't above using whatever means he had at his disposal to persuade her that it was a good idea. But first he had a little more business to attend to.

'As indisputably tragic as your story is, Mr Carr, I now have to ask you… Do you wish to complete the deal and have this money paid into your account today? Or, after hearing of your charming daughter's admirable concern for your welfare, have you changed your mind?'

As he came to the end of his question Ludo deliberately raised a wry eyebrow at Natalie, as if to demonstrate that he hadn't become a very rich man by being soft-hearted and swayed by every sob story that came his way. As much as he wanted to bed her, he wouldn't go back on the principles that had made him his fortune. Not for *anyone*…

CHAPTER FOUR

THE DEAL WAS signed. And, although Natalie refused to meet Ludo's enigmatic glance as she, her father and his solicitor started to file out of the traditionally furnished office, with its leaded diamond-shaped windowpanes and lingering scent of beeswax, she couldn't help regretting that the much anticipated dinner date with him tonight wasn't going to happen after all.

How could it after he'd so coldly refused her heartfelt plea to help her father by increasing his offer for the hotel chain? It was evident that making money was far more important to him than helping his fellow man. *Good riddance*, she thought, deliberately averting her gaze as she swept past him. But just the same her heart hammered hard as the warmth from his body mingled with the alluring scent of his aftershave and disturbingly reached out to arouse her.

'Natalie?'

To her astonishment he lightly wrapped his hand round her slender-boned wrist.

'I'd like a word with you, if I may?'

Before she could register anything but the sensation of his warm grip against her flesh and the glittering cobalt blue of his eyes he removed his hand and turned to address his waiting colleagues.

'I need some time alone with Ms Carr.' There was a definite tone of command in his voice and immediately they all stood up and filed out behind Natalie's dad and his solicitor.

Before Ludo could shut the door behind them Bill Carr returned, to plant himself in the doorway, a perturbed expression on his long lean face.

'May I ask why you want to talk to my daughter alone? If you're angry that she was a little outspoken on my behalf, please don't take it personally. I'm sure she meant no offence, Mr Petrakis,' he apologised.

Natalie found it hard to quell her annoyance that her father was being so meek. For God's sake—he almost sounded subservient! One thing she was sure of: *she* wouldn't be following suit...

'Don't worry, Mr Carr. Although your daughter's outburst was somewhat ill-advised, you can rest assured that I did not take it personally. I simply want to have a quiet word with her in private—if she is in agreement?'

Beginning to feel like a piece of property being bartered, Natalie bristled. Folding her arms across the cerise blouse she'd thrown into her tote at the last minute, she made herself meet Ludo's wry glance head-on, without giving in to the urge to demonstrate her annoyance and deliberately look away.

'Whatever it is you want to say to me, Mr Petrakis, you had better make it quick. I want to get to the bank before it closes.'

'No doubt to check that your father's money has gone

into his account?' Ludo commented coolly, lifting a lightly mocking eyebrow.

How she refrained from slapping his smooth, sculpted cheek Natalie didn't know.

'My father's money is nothing to do with me. Believe it or not, I do have my own bank account.'

He grinned disconcertingly. 'I'm very glad to hear it. Why don't you come and sit down for a minute so we can talk?'

Turning towards her father, thinking he must be wondering what on earth was going on between the two of them, she just about managed a reassuring smile. 'I'm sure this won't take long, Dad. Will you wait for me outside?'

'I'll meet you in the coffee shop across the road. Goodbye, Mr Petrakis.'

'It has been a pleasure doing business with you, Mr Carr.'

As soon as Natalie's puzzled dad had closed the door behind him she could no longer stem her irritation at the handsome Greek. 'What on *earth* can you possibly have to say to me after what you've just done? Whatever it is, I'm not sure I want to hear it. Unless you want me to convey to my dad your sincere apologies for being so heartlessly mercenary, I'd rather not waste any more time today hoping that a man who is deaf, dumb and blind to pleas for understanding will change his mind and be more compassionate. I think I'd rather put the whole thing down to bitter experience and be on my way.'

The expression on Ludo's face suddenly reflected a

severe winter frost. 'Your indignant attitude beggars belief. What just went on between your father and me was a business transaction—pure and simple. If you can't see that then you are more naive than I thought. It is clear that you have *no* idea about the vagaries of buying and selling, not to mention the effect of current market forces. If perhaps not the most successful businessman in the world, your father is at least a pragmatist and he does understand these things. I am sure he realises how fortunate he is to have had me make an offer for his business at all. It is not as though he was exactly overrun with them... At least now he will be able to pay off some of his debts.'

Natalie was shocked. 'How do *you* know about his debts?'

'I make it a point to investigate the credentials of anyone who hopes to sell me anything, Natalie.' Emitting a weary-sounding sigh, Ludo rubbed his hand round his lean, cut-glass jaw. 'I am genuinely sorry that your father has got himself into such a mess financially, but that does not mean I should be responsible for helping to get him out of it. I too have business interests to maintain.'

'I'm sure you do.'

Even though his chastising reply had irked and irritated her, Natalie had to admit that she had no right to berate him when her father had brought this whole unfortunate situation down on himself. He was right. Ludo *wasn't* responsible for her father's inability to hold on to his once successful business because he'd become distracted by his propensity for acquiring more and more unhelpful bad habits. Should she really be angry at Ludo because he hadn't agreed to pay more for the hotel chain? After all, she knew for a fact that he wasn't a mean man. Hadn't he spontaneously paid for her rail ticket yesterday?

Curling some long strands of drifting hair agitatedly round her ear, she inhaled a steadying breath. No matter how much she tried to square it with herself, it was still hard to understand why a businessman as wealthy as Ludo couldn't extend a little more understanding and kindness towards a fellow entrepreneur when he was in trouble. Weren't the newspapers and the media always banging on about the need for businesses to be more ethical these days rather than solely profit-driven?

'Was that all you wanted to say to me?' she asked, perversely wishing that he would talk to her about far more interesting and perhaps *personal* things rather than business—just so that she could hear the sound of pleasure in his voice and store it in her memory.

Almost as if he'd read her mind, Ludo's deliberately slow, answering smile made her shiver. Inside Natalie's lace bra her nipples prickled hotly, just as if he had run his fingertips over them...

Gravel-voiced he replied, 'No. It isn't. Did you forget that you agreed to meet me for dinner tonight?'

'No...I didn't forget. But that was before I knew that you were the man buying my father's business.'

'What does that have to do with us meeting for dinner?'

Natalie's grey eyes widened in surprise that he should even have to ask. 'How do you think my dad would feel if he found out I'd gone out to dinner with you? He'd feel betrayed. He's already been through more than he can take without me adding to his problems.'

'It sounds like you don't believe that your own needs should be met, Natalie. Why is that, I wonder?'

'What needs are we talking about?'

Her face burned, because even as she posed the question she knew *exactly* what he meant. It was undeniable that Ludo Petrakis aroused her. He aroused her more than any other man she'd ever been attracted to before... And what took her breath away was that, going by the licentiously seductive look in his incredible blue eyes, he seemed to be having similar feelings. But it didn't make the situation any less awkward or uncomfortable.

Yes, her dad had made some very foolish errors concerning his business, and consequently lost everything he'd worked so hard for, but Natalie didn't want to appear as though she was deliberately punishing him by seeing Ludo. Somehow she had to find the strength to walk away from the man, no matter *how* much her senses clamoured for her to see him again.

She tossed her head in a bid to demonstrate that the particular needs he'd alluded to meant nothing in comparison to the more pressing one she still had on her mind. 'The only needs I have at the moment are for my father to recover from this crippling setback and return to full health so he can find the energy and the will to start over again. By the way—not that you'll care—did your investigations tell you that as well as losing his business he's about to lose his home, too? Anyway, the reason I have to get to the bank is not to check that your money's gone into his account but to get some money out to pay you back for the ticket you bought me on the train. Fortunately I have discovered that there's an emergency code I can use to get some cash from my account.'

'Forget about that. It's not important. As far as I'm concerned you don't owe me anything. Rather than have you pay me back for the ticket I'd much prefer to take you to dinner tonight and start to get to know you a little.'

Even though it was flattering that Ludo was being so persistent, Natalie couldn't help but frown.

'Didn't you hear what I said? I'm sorry, but I can't risk upsetting my dad by seeing you again. You might assume that he's taking it all rather well under the circumstances, but he's most definitely *not* coping.' She stroked a not quite steady hand down over her tunic. 'Look, I really do have to go now. But before I do there's one more thing I want to ask. Why didn't you tell me you were Greek when we met on the train? Especially after I told you that my mother came from Crete?'

In his mind, Ludo confronted a familiar wall that he was still reluctant to climb. He was proud of his heritage, but it had been three years since he'd last visited his homeland…three years since his beloved older brother Theo had perished in a boating accident off the coast of the private island that Ludo owned. It had been the darkest time of his life, and the aftermath of the tragic event had seen him spiralling into a pit of despair that he'd feared he might never get out of.

Instead of staying home to grieve with his family he'd left quite soon after the funeral, hoping to find relief from his despondency by increasing his international business interests, travelling everywhere round the globe *except* for his beloved Greece... His parents couldn't understand why he wouldn't come home. Whenever he spoke to his mother on the phone she'd plead and cry for him to return. But as far as Ludo was concerned he had disappointed her on two unforgivable counts, so he wouldn't. Not only had he been unable to provide her with evidence of a healthy romantic relationship and the prospect of a grandchild, worse— *much* worse than that—his brother had died holidaying on the beautiful island paradise that Ludo had bought himself, as a reward for attaining the success he'd so often dreamed of as a boy, ultimately so that his parents might see that he was as good and successful a man as Theo. Now they would never see that.

Momentarily glancing away from the beautiful clear grey eyes that were so avidly studying him, he endeavoured to keep his tone matter-of-fact. 'At the time I was more interested in finding out about you, Natalie. Don't women often make the complaint that men talk too much about themselves?'

'I don't know about that. I just thought you'd have been pleased to tell me where you came from.'

'Why *is* that? So we might have exchanged personal anecdotes and stories about our shared heritage?' Ludo heard a spike of irritation in his voice that he couldn't hide because he'd been inadvertently pushed into a corner. He hadn't spoken about his country of birth or what had happened to drive him away from it to anyone... not even trusted friends. If he wanted things to progress with Natalie he was probably going to have to talk about it now, whether he liked it or not. 'Sometimes a man in my position is apt to crave anonymity,' he continued. 'Whether that's about where he comes from or who he is. Besides, do you really think our only point of connection is the fact that each of us has a parent who is Greek?'

'Yesterday I might have thought so, if you'd admitted it.' Hugging her arms across her chest, Natalie frowned. 'But since then things have unfolded to connect us in a way I never could have imagined. When I walked into that room today and saw that it was you—the man I'd met on the train—I was lost for words. It was such a shock. Anyway, going back to yesterday, you helped me out by paying for my ticket and, whether you want me to or not, it matters to *me* that I pay you back.'

'If that's the case then perhaps you will start to see the sense in meeting me tonight after all?' Ludo interjected smoothly.

'I can't.'

'You mean you won't?'

'I mean I can't. Why won't you listen to what I'm saying?'

Pressing the pads of his fingertips against his brow, he lightly shook his head. 'I'm listening, Natalie, but perhaps I'm not giving you the response you're looking for because *you* are not giving me the one that *I* want.'

Her eyes flashed with irritation. 'And no doubt you always get what you want?'

She released an exasperated sigh and her lithe figure moved purposefully back towards the door. His heart thudding at the realisation that the opportunity to see her again might disappear from right under his nose unless he took action, Ludo thought fast. As an idea presented itself he mentally grabbed at it, as though it might vanish in the next instant unless he expressed it. The idea was perhaps a little preposterous, but it made a strange kind of sense. Ludo decided to take the plunge and go with it.

'Perhaps you won't be in such a hurry to leave if I tell you that I have a deal in mind that I'd like to talk to you about? A deal that would benefit your father as well as yourself,' he asserted calmly.

Riveted, she immediately pulled her hand away from the brass doorknob and turned to face him. 'What kind of a deal?'

Pacing a little, to help arrange his thoughts, Ludo took his time in answering. It had suddenly dawned on him that what he was about to propose would benefit *him* too. The concept didn't seem at all preposterous any more. In fact it might potentially be the solution he'd secretly longed for—a way out that might bring him some peace at last.

He stopped pacing to settle his gaze on the beautiful, inquisitive face in front of him. 'The deal I'm offering you is that I will increase what I paid for your father's business by half the amount again if you agree to come with me to Greece and play the role of my fiancée.'

Natalie turned as still as a statue, her stunned expression suggesting she wasn't entirely sure she'd heard him right. Her next words confirmed it. 'Would you mind repeating what you just said? I'm afraid I might have imagined it.'

'You didn't imagine it.' Willingly, he repeated his proposition.

'You really will increase the money you paid for the business if I travel to Greece with you and pretend to be your fiancée? Why would you want me to do such a bizarre thing?'

Shrugging a shoulder, Ludo sighed. 'It will perhaps not be as bizarre as you might think when I tell you my reasons,' he remarked.

'Go on, then.' Moistening her lips, she patiently waited for him to continue.

'My parents—in particular my mother—have long hoped that I will bring someone home that I am serious about. Someone who will help give them hope that they might one day have a grandchild.'

Noting the brief flash of alarm in Natalie's candid gaze, Ludo forced himself to press on regardless. He told himself she wouldn't still be standing there listening if the idea was absolutely abhorrent to her.

'Unfortunately I have not had a long-term relationship in a long time and, frankly, they are becoming despondent that I ever will. The situation has become sadly compounded by my only brother's death three years ago in a boating accident. Now I am their only son and heir. Unfortunately I have not been home since the funeral. I did not want to return until I could give them hope that the future was brighter than they had perhaps envisaged. I know it is a pretence, Natalie, but the intention behind it is a kind one. I promise you that if you can convincingly act the part of my fiancée while we are in Greece, when we return to the UK I will make sure you are richly rewarded.'

'But even if I should agree to the pretence, how hurt will your parents be when they find out that the whole thing was a lie? They must be broken-hearted as it is to have lost their son. Nothing you can do for me or give me would make up for how terrible I'd feel about deceiving them.'

'The fact that you care so much about that aspect of the deal assures me that you are the right woman to ask this favour of, Natalie. I will be forever in your debt if you do this for me.'

She looked to be thinking hard for a moment. 'And how do I explain to my father that I am going away with you to Greece for—for how long?'

'At least three to four weeks, *paidi mou*.'

The soft pink hue that tinted her cheeks at his use of the Greek endearment momentarily distracted him, because it brought a lustre to her eyes that was nothing less than magical and gave him an irresistible glimpse of how she might look if he were to try and seduce her... prettily flushed and aroused. A little buzz of pleasurable heat ricocheted through his insides. He suddenly became even more determined to have Natalie masquerade as his fiancée... Especially as—in the hope of convincing his parents—he fully intended to play the part of devoted fiancé to the hilt.

'You can tell him that I have offered you the chance to learn the ropes of good financial dealing with an expert,' he asserted with a teasing smile. 'I am sure he will see the benefits of such an opportunity. If you take it, and learn what I consider to be the essential skills for success in business, your father will need to have no worries about your financial future, because you will know exactly how to go about securing it.'

As he came to the end of this speech Natalie moved across the room to a burgundy-coloured wing-backed armchair and slowly sank down into it. When she glanced up again to meet his eyes, Ludo experienced a private moment of undeniable triumph and relief, because suddenly he knew she was giving the offer serious consideration.

CHAPTER FIVE

WAS SHE CRAZY to consider Ludo's incredible suggestion that she go with him to Greece and assume the identity of his fiancée? It would fulfil her longed-for desire to visit Greece again, but the most important aspect of the deal he was proposing was that he'd promised to increase what he had paid to her father for his business.

Half the amount again would allow her dad to keep his flat and not be forced to sell it. The fact that he could keep his home would go a long way, Natalie believed, to helping him make a new start. Not only that, it might give his health a real boost too. This deal Ludo was proposing was too important to dismiss, she realised. How could she live with herself if she didn't take it and her dad's health and self-esteem sank even lower because he'd lost all hope in making things better for himself?

But now, as she let her gaze roam over the strikingly handsome man silently observing her, with his chiselled good looks and piercing blue eyes, a nervous cartwheel flipped in the pit of her stomach. Could she really contemplate playing the part of his fiancée? Would she be strong enough to pull it off without letting her feelings get involved? Being in close proximity with Ludo in

Greece and pretending to be his fiancée would surely mean holding hands, kissing and touching, perhaps *intimately…*

Natalie didn't allow her thoughts to venture any further, because they had already induced a powerful wave of heat that made her body feel as if it were near to bursting into flames. Lifting the heavy swathe of long hair off the back of her neck in a bid to help cool her temperature, she noticed that Ludo's previously confident expression had altered. Now his glance was more contemplative, as if he wasn't entirely sure that her response would be the one he hoped for. If that were true, Natalie wondered how such an amazingly successful and attractive man could ever be plagued by doubt of any kind. It didn't make sense.

'Well?'

He was levelling his gaze upon her a little more intently, and she got the impression his patience was wearing thin.

'Are you going to give me an answer to what I have proposed? Is it to be yes or no, Natalie?'

Sucking in a breath, she pushed to her feet. 'You make it sound so simple…to just say yes or no.'

'Are you saying it's more complicated?'

'Where emotions are involved no situation is ever going to be straightforward.'

'Why should emotions be involved?' Frowning in puzzlement, Ludo dug his hand into his trouser pocket. 'Are you worrying about your father and his reaction when he learns you're going to come to Greece with me? I shouldn't imagine it will be a problem, considering I have offered to increase the amount I paid him.'

Her heartbeat accelerating, Natalie felt herself redden. 'Actually, it's not my father I was worrying about. I don't have any doubt he'll be more than pleased with your new offer for the business, and as for me going to Greece with you—he'll accept it if he knows it's what I want, too. I was just wondering how, if I should go with you, I'm going to cope with playing your fiancée when we've only just met and I hardly know you? Aren't engaged couples supposed to behave as though they're crazy about each other?'

Ludo's amused smile emphasised his even white teeth and sexy, sun-kissed tan. She caught her breath.

'Do you think you will find it difficult to pretend that you're crazy about me, *paidi mou*? Most women I know tell me I am quite a catch. Some have even called me "irresistible"… Shall we put the theory to the test?'

Before Natalie realised his intention he walked right up to her and encircled her waist. Being up close and personal with his body as he pulled her towards him, smelling the alluring musky aftershave he wore, made her knees come very close to folding even before he embraced her. A stunned gasp left her throat as he lowered his head and kissed her. As soon as his lips made contact she opened her mouth and he expertly inserted his smooth, silken tongue inside to make the kiss even more intimate.

Every thought in her head vanished except the one that registered the fierce addictive pleasure of his taste and the sexy heated brand of his skin against hers. It felt as though a torch had ignited an unforgettable flame in her blood that no other man before or after him could ever hope to compete with… In the silence of her mind a renegade response came. *Okay…I'll cope. It can't be that difficult.*

She enjoyed the kiss so much she was genuinely disappointed when Ludo eased the delightful pressure on her lips. Lifting his head to gaze down at her, he moved his hands from her waist to rest them lightly on her hips. Up close, his stunning sapphire eyes were matchlessly blue, like a sunlit Mediterranean sea in midafternoon. Even his dark blond lashes were impossibly lavish. It didn't matter if he were rich or poor, Natalie decided. The man's physical assets were simply amazing.

'Hmm…' He smiled. 'That was nice.'

She hoped he wouldn't want a more detailed assessment from her on how *she* felt about the kiss. She might just have to tell him she'd like to try another one, just to make sure she hadn't imagined the spine-tingling pleasure it had given her.

'Can I take it that the idea of playing my fiancée is not as repellent as you might have thought initially?' he teased softly.

Natalie couldn't help but be honest. 'I'm sure you know that you're far from repellent. But it still doesn't make it easy for me to pretend I'm something that I'm not. I feel very uneasy about deceiving anyone, even in a good cause. Especially your parents.'

Reaching towards her, Ludo moved some silken strands of hair away from her face and gently stroked his hand down over her cheekbone. 'Because you are naturally such a thoughtful person I know they won't have a problem accepting you as my girlfriend,' he asserted confidently.

'A girlfriend is one thing...I could cope with that. But introducing me as your fiancée is much more serious, don't you think?'

Removing his hand from her cheek, he expelled a heavy sigh. The quirk at the corner of his exquisitely carved mouth suggested some exasperation. 'Think of it as a harmless game of "Let's Pretend". Believe me when I say that you are not hurting anybody. After all, you will be getting what you want for your father, remember? That and an opportunity to visit your mother's country...something you told me you'd love to do again.'

Stepping away from him so that she might think straight, Natalie knew she had to make a decision. She sent up a silent prayer that it was the right one.

'All right, then. I'll do as you ask and go to Greece with you. But if when I'm there it becomes in any way difficult or untenable for me to keep up the charade of being your fiancée then do you agree I can go home, no questions asked?'

Somewhat reluctantly Ludo nodded his head. 'I will not be happy about it, but I will agree so long as you remember I am paying your father a great deal of money for his business. You at least owe me the courtesy of staying with me until I tell you I am satisfied.'

'Satisfied?' The hot colour started at the tips of Natalie's toes and travelled in an all-consuming heatwave right up to her scalp. The word *satisfied* had many connotations, so why did she have to focus on the sexual one first? Transfixed by Ludo's shimmering blue gaze, she didn't have to search very hard for the answer.

'Yes—satisfied that you have acted the part of my fiancée to the very best of your ability and played it as convincingly as possible.'

'I'm no actress. I can only do the best I can. All right, then.' Briefly withdrawing her gaze, she glanced down at the polished wooden floor to help regain her equilibrium, because her heart was thudding alarmingly at the daunting prospect of what she was agreeing to do. 'You'd better tell me when you're intending to travel.'

'As far as I'm concerned, the sooner the better. Could you be ready to go in a week's time?'

'That *is* soon. I'll need to arrange help at the B&B for my mum while I'm away. I hope a week will be enough time for me to organise things.'

'You have already intimated to me that you are a good organiser, Natalie. I'm sure a week will give you plenty of time. You should be ready to leave next Monday, when I intend us to travel on an early-morning flight. As we will be departing from Heathrow you should probably arrange to stay with your father the night before.'

'I'm sure that won't be a problem.'

'I'm sure it won't.' With a mocking glint in his eye, Ludo drolly echoed her comment. 'Especially when he learns that I am not as uncharitable and hard-hearted as you both first suspected.'

'I never meant to deliberately insult you by what I said. I was just upset, as any loving daughter would be, at the prospect of my dad struggling to get by after paying all his debts. It seemed so unfair that after being forced to sell his business after so many dedicated years of hard work the proceeds wouldn't even leave him enough to live on.'

Even though she had felt entirely justified, Natalie was still embarrassed at being reminded of her accusatory outburst at the meeting.

Flushing, she glanced briefly down at her watch and declared, 'I really do have to go now—but there's just one more thing I need to say before I leave.' Her teeth nibbled anxiously at her lip. 'I'm really sorry to hear about your brother. Such a dreadful loss must have been devastating for you and your family…I really feel for you all.'

A shadow seemed to move across Ludo's bright blue irises, momentarily darkening them. 'Devastating is not a big enough word,' he murmured, awkwardly dragging his fingers through his thick fair hair. 'But I appreciate your sympathy.'

'Well, I think it's time I left. Presumably you'll ring me when you have the flight times?'

'You can count on it.' Moving with her towards the door, Ludo lightly touched her arm. 'But I won't just be contacting you then. I'm going to ring you during the week—preferably in the evenings, when I'm not working. I think it's quite important that we get to know each other a little before our trip, don't you?'

'Talking to each other on the phone is hardly the best way to get to know someone, but I suppose it will have to do if we can't see each other.'

'As much as I would like to, it's impossible for me

to free up any time to see you this week, Natalie. For now, phone calls will have to suffice.'

Meeting his enigmatic gaze, she could do no more than shrug in agreement, even though in truth she was disappointed. It was a mystery to her how Ludo had got under her skin so quickly. She'd never experienced such a tangible sense of connection with a man before, and everything that she believed about herself had been turned on its head.

'Okay. I'll expect your calls later on in the week, then,' she murmured.

'Good. By the way, when we arrive in Rhodes the weather should be seasonally hot. Bring plenty of suitable clothing and sun-cream,' he suggested.

The sociable smile that accompanied his words was far warmer than she'd expected after the sorrow he'd just expressed about the loss of his brother, and Natalie was already nursing a secret hope that he might talk about his sibling more fully during their time together in Greece. There was so much about this complex, surprising man that she longed to discover.

'I will.'

She couldn't help feeling shy all of a sudden, and curled her palm round the brass doorknob, then swept out of the office into the reception area—only to be confronted by the curious glances of Ludo's colleagues.

After giving her father the good news that Ludo had increased the sum he had paid for the business, and hearing that he was much more optimistic about his future because of it, the following day Natalie returned home

to Hampshire. Trepidation, hope and great doubt accompanied her.

First and foremost, she could hardly believe that she'd
agreed to go to Greece with Ludo in just a week's time
and endeavour to convince his parents that they were
engaged. Surely they would know immediately that an
unremarkable girl like her was the least likely woman
he would choose as a fiancée? For a start, she was a million miles away from the perfect-looking women who
adorned the arms of rich and powerful men like their
son in the glossy magazines.

But the following evening when Ludo phoned, trepidation and doubt instantly fled to be replaced by a totally unexpected wild optimism and hope. All it took
was hearing the sound of his rich baritone voice.

Without preamble he announced, 'It's me—Ludo.'

About to take a bath, Natalie grasped the white bathsheet she'd wrapped round her torso to make it more secure, just as if he'd suddenly appeared in the room and
his arresting cobalt gaze was resting on her semi-naked
form. Dropping down onto the bed, she sent up a fervent
prayer that her voice wouldn't betray how strongly his
call had affected her. Despite agreeing to go to Greece
with him, it felt somehow surreal that the handsome
businessman should call her personally.

'Hi,' she answered, the nerves she'd hoped she'd ban-
ished already alarmingly evident. 'How are you?'

'Tired and very much in need of a holiday.'

The surprisingly unguarded reply took Natalie aback
and filled her with concern. 'Well, thankfully you don't

have too long to wait before you get away…just a few more days.'

'Presumably I don't need to check you *are* still coming with me?'

With thudding heart, Natalie said quickly, 'No, you don't need to check. When I give my word I keep it.'

'Good. Do you have a pen and paper at hand? I want to give you some flight details.'

When she'd written them down she asked, 'Is that all?'

'No.' She heard a disconcerting smile in his voice.

'I'd like to talk to you some more. What have you been doing with yourself today?'

Sighing, Natalie smoothed her hand down over the soft towelling nap of the bathsheet. Not that it remotely mattered, but if Ludo intended talking for much longer then her bathwater would be turning unpleasantly cold.

'What have I been doing? Helping to organise some help in the B&B while I'm away, and also seeing to some rather tedious administration, I'm afraid. But thankfully it was alleviated by my mum's baking. Just after three she brought me in some homemade scones and jam with a cup of tea. No one in the world makes scones as melt-in-the-mouth and tasty as she does!'

'You have an extremely sexy voice, Natalie. I can't be the only man who's ever told you that.'

Dumbfounded, Natalie automatically shook her head, as if Ludo was indeed in the room. The only thing she could conjure up right then wasn't an answer but a mental picture of him smiling at her. The sculpted planes of his tanned cheekbones, chiselled jaw and intense

sapphire-coloured eyes were more than enough to drive
away any intelligible reply.

'Natalie? Are you still there?'

'Yes, I'm still here. But I ran a bath just before you
rang and it must be getting cold. I'm afraid I'll have
to go.'

On her feet, she carried her mobile to the slightly ajar
bathroom door and anxiously bit down on her lip as she
waited for his reply. The comment he'd made about her
having a sexy voice had unravelled her.

'Well, then, you must go and take your bath. But
know this… I don't think I'm going to be able to sleep
at all tonight, since I will have in my mind the arresting image of you naked, soaking in a bath of scented
bubbles. I hope when I ring again tomorrow night you'll
end the conversation on a far less provocative note?
Goodnight, Natalie. Sleep well.'

By the time Natalie had roused herself from the
trance she'd fallen into, her bathwater and the scented
bath foam she'd poured into it were too cold to contemplate immersing herself in. Resigning herself to going
without, she pulled out the plug and once again got lost
in thoughts of Ludo as she watched the water spiralling
urgently down into the drain…

It had been a far from easy journey to his homeland for
Ludo. The inner turmoil of his thoughts had made it
impossible for him to relax.

The private plane he'd chartered was the epitome
of the luxury he'd long come to expect when he travelled. As far as that was concerned there had been

nothing to complain about. The cabin crew had been ultra-professional and attentive, and the flight had been smooth without any disconcerting turbulence. But even though the sight of Natalie at the airport, in a pretty multicoloured maxi-dress, with her shining hair, had quickened his pulse, it had still been difficult to raise his spirits.

Ludo had immensely enjoyed and indeed looked forward to the nightly telephone conversations he'd had with Natalie, but when she'd sat beside him on the plane, every now and then attempting to engage him in light conversation, he hadn't found it easy to respond in the same cheerful fashion he'd been able to adopt on the phone. In fact his mood had deteriorated more and more the closer they'd got to their destination.

The phone conversation he'd had with his mother earlier that morning had been a double-edged sword. While it had been a joy to hear her voice, and to be able to relate some good news to her, it didn't assuage the onerous weight of guilt and pain that still dogged him over his brother's death. Clearly overwhelmed and excited about the prospect of seeing Ludo again after three long years, his mother had had an emotion in her voice that had almost made it hard for him to breathe, let alone speak. There had been no words of reprimand or blame to make him feel guiltier than he was already, and somehow that had made the prospect of seeing her and his father again even more difficult.

Naturally they'd wanted to send a car to bring him and Natalie back to their spacious villa, but Ludo had carefully and respectfully declined the offer. He'd told her that he and Natalie were going to stay at his own waterside villa and take a valuable day's rest before they drove out to see them. Even though his absence had been a prolonged one, he'd need a little more time to acclimatise himself to the fact that he was home again, as well as time to take stock.

His mother had naturally been curious about Natalie. 'What's she like?' she'd asked excitedly. 'Are you happy with her, my son?'

All Ludo had told her was that Natalie was a 'charming, good-natured girl' and that he was sure they would love her. He'd deliberately squashed down the wave of remorse that had crashed through him because he was inventing a scenario that wasn't true.

For some strange, inexplicable reason, at the back of his mind the tentative hope had surfaced that some good might come of being with Natalie despite his deception. He hadn't just enjoyed their nightly phone conversations, he had started to *rely* on them. She'd always been so reassuring, and if he'd had a bad day his spirits had been buoyed by the idea of talking to her. He'd never experienced such a strong connection to a woman before. And the memory of the sexy, ardent kiss that he'd shared with her back in his office a week ago had definitely got him believing that having her with him in Greece might help alleviate some of the stress that would inevitably come his way.

But he also knew it would take more than one kiss or a reassuring conversation to ease the grief and anxiety he was feeling about returning home again.

Finally, just before they'd reached the cosmopolitan

Greek island they were heading for, Natalie had shaken him out of his morose mood with an unexpected comment.

'As you know, I'm not undertaking this trip purely because I'm in love with the idea of going to Greece, or because I need a holiday. I'm doing it because you offered me a deal that was impossible to refuse. While I'm not exactly looking forward to playing your fiancée, I respect the fact that you paid my father a much more realistic price for his business than you initially offered. And because of that I fully intend to honour my part of the bargain. However, it's a little off-putting that you don't seem to want to talk to me. If it's because you're having second thoughts about bringing me with you, I want you to know that I'm perfectly willing to get on the next flight home just as soon as it can be arranged.'

It was as though she'd dashed a bucket full of ice water in his face. For one thing, it didn't do his ego a whole lot of good to hear her confess that she wasn't looking forward to playing his fiancée and was willing to go home if he'd changed his mind. Turning in his seat, he studied the troubled but defiant expression on the lovely face before him with a stab of remorse.

'That is most definitely *not* what I'd prefer, *paidi mou*. Forgive me for not being a more amiable companion. It is nothing to do with my not wanting to be with you. It is purely a private dilemma that has been preoccupying me.'

Folding her hands in her lap across the pretty colourful fabric of her dress, Natalie lifted her huge grey eyes to his. 'Is that dilemma to do with returning to

Greece for the first time since your brother died? The last thing I want to do is distress you by asking you to talk about it, but don't you think it would help us both if you opened up a little? I'm sure it's going to seem very strange to your parents if I haven't got a clue about what your brother was like or how you felt about him.'

Ludo stared. What she said was perfectly true. He now saw that he hadn't given his impromptu plan nearly enough consideration. As painful and uncomfortable as it might be, he had no choice but to talk to Natalie about Theo.

Linking his hands together, he felt his heart race a little as he attempted to marshal his thoughts. 'Very well, then. I will tell you something of my brother Theo. Where do I begin? He was a giant of a man—our very own Rhodes Colossus… Not just in build—he was six foot four—but in character and heart too. Ever since he went to medical school to train as a doctor he knew he wanted to specialise in taking care of children.' He allowed himself a briefly strained smile. 'So that's what he did. He became a paediatrician. At the clinics he attended, or on the wards, the kids just loved him. More than that, when he told them he would make them better they totally believed him…as did their parents. More often than not he was able to keep that heartfelt promise. Pretty soon his services were in demand not just in Greece but all over Europe.'

Natalie's answering smile was unreserved and encouraging. 'It sounds as though he was quite a man. You and your parents must have been so proud of him.

'Everyone was. He might have been my brother, but it was a privilege to know him, let alone be related to him.'

'Was he married? Did he have children of his own?'

The flush of pink that Ludo realised was a given whenever she was remotely embarrassed or self-conscious was very much in evidence again.

'No.' He hefted a sigh. 'He used to tell us all he was married to his work. He may not have been a father biologically, but he was father to many children when they were in his care.'

'I wish I'd been able to meet him.'

'If you had, you would never have given me a second glance.' The painfully wry comment was expressed before Ludo had a chance to check it.

Natalie's perfectly arched brows lifted in bewilderment. 'Why would you say that? You must know you have many appealing qualities—and I'm not referring to your wealth.'

'My brother was admired for his kind and unselfish nature as well as his desire to help heal children afflicted by illness or disability. Compared to him, my own achievements are a lot less worthy and nowhere near in the same league.'

'I can't believe you mean that. Not everyone has the skill of creating wealth like you do, Ludo—wealth that no doubt helps create jobs and opportunity—and I'm sure a lot of people wish they had. I don't doubt your family is as proud of you as of the son they sadly lost.'

'My parents will tell you they are, but my brother was a tough act to follow. He was a son in a million... irreplaceable.'

Natalie fell silent. The sadness in her eyes took Ludo aback. He regretted being so candid with her. He had never craved anyone's sympathy and never would, yet her unstinting kindness undid him.

Quickly searching for a new topic to divert her, he said, 'I should have asked you this before, but how did your parents take the news you were coming on this trip with me?'

He was disturbed by the idea that she might have put herself in an awkward position with her family. He didn't want them to give her a hard time over it. No doubt it would taint the experience for her if they did. Where he came from family were the number one priority, and he completely understood Natalie's devotion to her own. Clearly she didn't want to worry or shame them by taking off with a man they didn't even know. Even her father had only met him that one time in his office, and the occasion would hardly have let him warm to Ludo in any way.

As he silently observed her, Ludo felt his heartbeat quicken at the increasing evidence of her thoughtful and caring nature. It didn't hurt that she was rather beautiful too… To his surprise, the dour mood that had plagued him since the start of the trip lightened.

'My dad was very worried at first,' Natalie confessed. 'When I told him you'd substantially increased what you paid for the business he feared you'd only done it to try and blackmail me into becoming your lover.'

Her porcelain cheeks suddenly acquired the most radiant shade of pink Ludo had ever seen. But, surprisingly, he found he wasn't offended by the idea that her father had feared he was blackmailing his daughter, because he understood the older man's natural concern. It would surely take a hard-hearted father *not* to be concerned. Ludo was pleased that Natalie had frankly admitted it, because it gave him the opportunity to set her straight.

'I have been known to be ruthless in my bid to seal a deal, but I am no blackmailer, Natalie. Besides, does your father really think I'd need to resort to that in order to make you my lover?' Gently touching her lips with his fingertips, he was intrigued to know her response. 'I wouldn't, would I, Natalie?'

CHAPTER SIX

HER EYES WIDENED to incandescent twin full moons.

'Of course you wouldn't. I'm quite capable of making up my own mind about whether I take a man as a lover or not, without being coerced by the promise of money or—or whatever.'

Frowning and pursing her lips, she let her long hair slip silkily round her face, as though to shield her from closer scrutiny, and it made Ludo want to brush it back for her with his fingers. He would have done exactly that had she not started talking again.

'I told him I thought that despite your wealth and position you were most likely a decent man. I told him you'd suggested that if I spent some time with you in Greece I could benefit from learning important business skills that would help me in the future.'

'And you didn't mention that I'd asked you to assume the role of my fiancée?'

Hectic colour once again suffused her features. 'No…I thought it best not to mention that part.'

'I'm not sure whether I should take your declaration about me as being "most likely" a "decent man" as a compliment or not. The way you said it leaves me with the feeling that perhaps you doubt it.'

'I don't.'

In her haste to reassure him Natalie automatically laid her hand over his. Never before had the simple touch of a woman's hand inflamed Ludo to the point of wanting to haul her onto his lap and make love to her there and then, but that was what he felt at the sensation of her cool soft skin against his and the alluring drift of her pretty perfume.

'Even though you said you didn't want me to pay you back,' she continued, 'I haven't forgotten your generosity in paying for my train fare. Not many people would have been so quick to help out a complete stranger, and that absolutely illustrates how decent you are.'

The tension in his shoulders started to ease. He wouldn't normally care what a woman thought of his character if he was contemplating taking her to bed, but with Natalie he found he definitely craved her good opinion. The nightly phone calls they'd shared had played a big part in changing his attitude, especially when she'd talked about being concerned for family and friends, even the guests who stayed at the bed and breakfast. Her store of kindness knew no limits, it seemed.

'I confess to being reassured. What about your mother? What did she think of you going to Greece with me?' he asked interestedly. 'Did you tell her who I was, *glykia mou*?'

'Yes, I did.'

'And what did she say?'

To Ludo's great disappointment, she withdrew the

slim hand that still lay over his and lightly shrugged a shoulder.

'She told me to be careful...then she told me to tell you that she was very sorry to hear about your brother. She'd heard of him, you see. She told me about his reputation for being an incredible paediatrician and that the Greek community held him in the highest regard.'

Learning that Natalie's mother was Greek had been one thing. But discovering that she'd heard of his brother as well as of his shocking demise was deeply unsettling. He was also disturbed that she'd advised her beautiful daughter to 'be careful'. She could only mean one thing. Presumably, in her eyes, Ludo wasn't held in the same high regard as his brother had been. *No change there, then.* His lighter mood evaporated like ice beneath a burning sun.

'Hopefully that will reassure her that you are in good hands,' he commented dryly, 'even though it sounds like she mistrusts me. Why else would she warn you to be careful?'

'Every mother who cares about her grown-up daughter worries about who they're associating with... especially when it comes to men.'

'Well, my beautiful Natalie, I will do my best to allay her fears and send you home completely intact.'

Smiling ruefully, he signalled to the male flight attendant standing nearby and without hesitation ordered a glass of Remy Martin brandy.

On their arrival at his stunning waterside villa, Ludo's housekeeper Allena and her husband Christos came out to greet them. As he found himself embraced by two of the warmest hugs he'd had in a very long time Ludo was almost overcome by the couple's genuine pleasure at seeing him again. It made him realise just how much he'd missed their familiar faces and unreserved regard.

They were a little more politely restrained when he introduced them to Natalie, but their smiles couldn't hide their pleasure and curiosity. *He didn't doubt they'd heard on the grapevine that he was bringing his fiancée home.* As a wave of guilt descended yet again, he filed it away irritably and refused to think about it. Wasn't it enough that he'd fulfilled his parents' wishes and come home?

After Allena had told him that she'd prepared something special for their dinner that night, and that there were cool drinks waiting for them out on the terrace, Christos lifted their luggage from the car and he and his wife transported it into the villa to dispatch it to their rooms. Relieved that he could have Natalie to himself for a while, in the privacy of his own home, Ludo guided her through the open-plan living room out onto the large terrace to take in the view. He couldn't deny the sense of pride it gave him to know that she would adore it.

The shimmering azure sea glinting in the midafternoon sun just a few feet from the door was like a sheet of sparkling glass it was so still and perfect. And the warm scented breeze that blew in to caress her skin was infused with the most heavenly scent of bougainvillaea. With delight Natalie saw that the radiant red and pink flowers were generously draped over every dazzling white wall in sight. It was hard to believe she hadn't wandered into a dream. For a long time she had yearned to come back to Greece, and to find herself here in this breathtaking idyll with a man as handsome and charismatic as Ludo Petrakis made the experience seem even more like the most incredible fantasy.

'What a gorgeous view! It's just wonderful! It's even more stunning than I'd hoped it would be,' she breathed, letting her hands rest on the sun-warmed railing of the stone-pillared balustrade.

Her companion smiled fleetingly. 'Many people call it the Jewel of the Aegean.'

'It must be,' Natalie concurred.

Ludo shook his head. 'Personally, I think that title should go to *my* island.'

'What do you mean, *your* island?' She wasn't sure why, but underneath her ribs Natalie's heart bumped a little faster. It was already racing due to Ludo's enigmatic smile. Her only regret was that she wished his smiles weren't quite so rare...

'It is called Margaritari, which is the Greek word for pearl.'

'That's beautiful. And this island? It's somewhere that you're particularly fond of?'

His chiselled profile was facing out to sea as she asked him this, and a sudden breeze lifted some dark golden strands from his hair and blew them across his forehead. As Natalie stared, mesmerised, a muscle flinched in the side of his carved cheekbone and he went very still.

'I was so enamoured of it that I bought it. Sadly, I

am not so enamoured of it any more, since my brother died there in the boating accident.'

As she reeled from the shocking admission Ludo left her side to make his way to a cane chair positioned next to a slatted wooden table and sat down.

'I hardly know what to say.' Immediately she moved to the other side of the table, so that she could see his expression. 'What a devastating blow for the accident to have happened on the waters of your own island.'

It was almost unbearable to think of Ludo being consumed not only by grief but also by guilt. Did he blame himself for the accident? Was that why he sometimes looked so troubled and didn't believe he was as well regarded as his brother Theo had been?

'It was…it *is*.' He didn't bother to try and disguise the painful emotion that gripped him. It was written all over his face. 'I had often urged him to take a holiday and make free with the island for as long as he wanted. It is so private there that only people I personally invite are allowed to stay. It is a magical place, and I'd hoped it would work its magic on him and help him relax. He rarely took time off from his work and my parents often expressed their concern that he looked so tired.'

Restless again, Ludo shot to his feet and strode round the table. He stopped directly in front of Natalie, and the look in his diamond-chipped blue eyes was so full of torment it made her catch her breath.

'He finally took up the offer and went to stay there. One day he took a boat out and it capsized. It was hard to understand how it had happened… Theo was a good sailor. But I found out afterwards that there were strong gusts of wind that day. Apparently they must have caught the mast and turned the boat over before he could do anything about it. He was a good swimmer, but the coroner told us that if he had been particularly fatigued his reactions would have been slow, and that's why he had been dragged under the boat and drowned.'

'Ludo, I'm so sorry…really I am.'

'A thing like that…a loss so grievous…the pain of it never goes away.'

It was a purely humanitarian instinct to offer comfort that made Natalie bridge the short distance between them and embrace him. At first she sensed his body turn rigid as the trunk of an oak, immovable, with no give or softness in it whatsoever. Her stomach sank to her boots as she thought she'd done the wrong thing. But before she could retreat self-consciously Ludo captured her shoulders and crushed her lips beneath his in a searing, passionate kiss that stole her breath and rendered her limbs weak as a new-born babe's.

The leap of unexpected raw desire that shot through her in response was like a lightning bolt appearing out of a cloudless blue summer sky. She emitted a hungry groan that she could scarce believe was her. It was coupled with a delicious languorous ache that suddenly stole over her like a fever, and Natalie couldn't help but kiss him back with equal ardour, loving the feel of his hard, honed body beneath her explorative fingers so much that she didn't at first register his palm spreading over her breast or sense that he was aroused.

Stunned that she'd let things progress quite so far, she immediately started to draw away. But Ludo held her fast, lifting his head to gaze down at her with a sensual, rueful smile that made her heart thump hard.

'Where do you think you are going?'

The commanding tenor of his captivating voice made it impossible for her to move.

'I shouldn't have done that.' Even though she'd intended to withdraw, his languuourous sexy gaze continued to transfix her.

With his hands now resting lightly on her hips, Ludo made no concession to the comment other than to subject her to a provocative study of her eyes and lips.

'You did absolutely the right thing, *paidi mou*. Make no mistake about that. I was in a dark place and your warm, very welcome embrace brought me out into the light.'

'Then I don't regret it.' Proffering a tentative smile, Natalie found she could neither move nor look away, and didn't wish that she could.

'That pleases me very much.' His hand reached out to capture a long strand of her glossy brown hair and he wound it round and round his fingers, as though mesmerised by the treasure he'd found.

If his housekeeper hadn't appeared on the patio just then Natalie wondered how long he would have kept her there, just playing with her hair and staring at her as if he'd like to do so much more...

'Excuse me, Mr Petrakis.' Allena's charming faltering English was no doubt in deference to his guest. 'Your rooms are ready.'

'*Efharisto,* Allena,' Ludo replied, reluctantly freeing the coil of hair he'd captured and stepping round to Natalie's side.

Feeling her face grow hot at being caught out in what could have been a highly awkward situation, she turned slowly. Her lips still ached and throbbed from the passionate kisses she'd exchanged with Ludo, and the expensive musky cologne he used that smelled of pure sex clung to her skin, as though to ensure she would never forget the encounter. Just in time she remembered there was no need for any awkwardness or embarrassment as she was supposed to be Ludo's fiancée. But the inflammatory thought didn't help to cool the heat that still tumbled like an unstoppable raging river through her bloodstream...

'Come.'

Placing his hand beneath her elbow, the man at her side led her back into the pleasantly cool villa and up a flight of white marble stairs. Determinedly holding on to the fact that Allena had said 'rooms', and not 'room', Natalie tried not to feel so tense. Even though she found herself intensely attracted to Ludo, it was still overwhelming to imagine being in his bed. For one thing, her experience of such a scenario was extremely limited. In fact one might legitimately say it was non-existent. No wonder she was tense. And if that weren't enough to contend with tomorrow she would be introduced to his parents as his intended bride-to-be! What if they saw immediately that she was merely putting on an act and she was no such thing?

'This room is for you.'

Gesturing that she should enter the light and spacious

room ahead of him, Ludo was quiet as Natalie endeavoured to take in her luxurious surroundings. Her heart raced when her gaze fell on the imposing carved bed in front of her. With its sash curtaining of sumptuous gold silk and matching counterpane scattered with an array of scarlet and gold-braided cushions, it was a bed fit for a princess. More than that, Natalie thought, it was a bed created for the perfect *seduction*…

Realising that Ludo was intimately observing her reaction, she didn't let her gaze linger a moment longer than necessary on the imposing bed. Frowning, she examined the art on the walls instead. It didn't help matters when she saw that the framed scenes depicted some of the most sensually charged stories in Greek mythology. There was an elegant print of *The Awakening of Adonis* by John Waterhouse, and two skilfully executed oil paintings of the beautiful Aphrodite and Andromeda. Andromeda was depicted in the part of the legend where she was chained to the rocks before Perseus came to rescue her from the sea monster.

Studying the pictures of the two bare-breasted women, Natalie felt the blood slow and thicken in her veins as though it were treacle. Ever since she'd first laid eyes on Ludo she seemed to have developed a heightened awareness of her womanhood—of needs that had lain dormant for too long without true opportunity for release. It was extremely disconcerting that they should come to the fore now.

She turned away and a far less provocative scene met her gaze, utterly stilling the anxious thoughts dominating her mind just then. Emitting a heartfelt sigh of pure pleasure, she stared transfixed at the awe-inspiring vista presented before her. The generously proportioned French windows stood open to reveal the most breathtaking view of the sparkling, still aquamarine sea. An exquisite breeze imbued with the arresting tones of bougainvillaea and pine in drifted intoxicatingly just at that very moment. Overwhelmed at her good fortune in being able to experience such beautiful natural delights, Natalie turned round to share her joy with her host.

'I'm almost speechless. This is one of the most incredible views I've ever seen. I feel so lucky.' She smiled, then added quickly, 'To be here, I mean.' Her smile started to slide off of her face when she saw the knowing look in Ludo's arresting blue eyes.

'Because you are here with me or because you have fallen in love with my country?' he teased.

'I've always been in love with Greece,' she murmured, crossing her arms over the soft linen bodice of her dress. 'This is my mother's country too, remember?'

'I did not forget, my angel. Did you think I had?'

He had gradually been moving towards her as he spoke, and now he stood in front of her with a scorching glance hot enough to melt her innermost core. Nervously, Natalie smoothed a less than steady hand down the front of her dress. 'You said—you told me that this was my room? I have to ask...do you intend to share it?'

'No, Natalie, I do not.' His flawless blue eyes glinted enigmatically. 'The only room you will share with me—and then only if you invite yourself—is *mine*. It is right next door to this one and the door will always be open during the night, should you feel inclined to visit me, *glykia mou.*'

It wasn't what she had expected him to say at all. For a long moment, even though her mind teemed with all the possible reasons she could think of as to why he didn't simply announce he was expecting her to act like his fiancée from day one and sleep with him— especially after their explosive kiss downstairs—Ludo's matter-of-fact answer perturbed her.

'That's fine,' she answered tetchily, immediately on the defensive. 'As long as you don't take it for granted that I *will* visit you.' Two hot flags of searing heat scorched her cheeks. 'We are only *pretending* to be engaged after all.'

Chuckling softly, Ludo lightly pushed back the slightly waving strand of hair that glanced against her cheekbone, and the movement reacquainted her with the tantalising drift of his provocative cologne.

'What a charming young woman you are, *glykia mou.* Yet, charming as you are, I hasten to remind you that we made a bargain, did we not?'

Lifting her chin, Natalie scowled, even as her heart thundered at her own daring. 'Yes, we did. But as far as I can recall our bargain didn't involve casual sex. We only agreed that I would come to Greece with you and *pretend* to be your fiancée. There was nothing said about our having intimate relations.'

'Are you saying that you are not attracted to me?'

'Clearly, after the kiss we shared downstairs, that would be a lie. But just because I find you attractive it doesn't mean I'm going to sleep with you at the drop of a hat!'

'No…?'

Even as he sardonically uttered the word Ludo overpowered her with an ardent embrace and once again captured her lips. As her mouth opened to receive the hot invasion of his tongue and his arms possessively encircled her narrow waist Natalie couldn't help whimpering with pleasure. Immediately his action acquainted her with the intoxicating heat radiating through his linen shirt, as well as the steely hardness of his strong, hard-muscled body. If he continued to drug her into submission with his arousing kisses, much as she secretly revelled in the seductive attention, she realised she wouldn't have a prayer of denying him that nocturnal visit—and the implications of such an action *terrified* her.

Dragging her lips determinedly away, she tried to shape what she hoped was a blasé smile. 'Do you think I might have some time to myself to unpack? Perhaps when I'm done I could join you for that cool drink your housekeeper said was out on the terrace?'

'You certainly know how to drive a hard bargain, angel. Was that your intention? To drive me crazy with desire so that I will give you anything you ask for?'

'You make it sound like I have some kind of plan. I definitely don't. The only reason I'm here at all is because you agreed to pay my father a fairer price for his business. You kept your end of the bargain before we left England and now I'm keeping mine. Other than that

I have no expectations…except perhaps to enjoy a holiday. It's been a long time since I've had a proper break.'

The stunning Adonis in front of her threw up his hands in frustration. 'Then go and unpack your things and meet me out on the terrace as soon as you can. Just so that you know—my own intention is to monopolise every moment of your time while you are here, Natalie…so much so that when the time comes for you to leave the very notion of parting from me and my country will break your heart!'

Striding to the door, he didn't spare her a single glance before angrily departing. Staring after him, Natalie moved over to the sumptuous silk-covered bed and sank down onto it, clutching her hands over her chest in bewilderment and shock.

He was not a man to be easily subdued when frustrated. When a long cold shower didn't help temper his thwarted desire, Ludo strode out onto the private balcony adjacent to his bedroom in an attempt to lose himself in the breathtaking Mediterranean view that for the past three years he had denied himself. Vying with the tantalising images of Natalie he had in his mind, memories of his childhood and youth inevitably came flooding back.

Inhaling a deep breath, he endeavoured to get a better grip on his emotions. He had just started to relax a little when on the horizon glinting in the sunshine he glimpsed a small white sailing vessel. It was about the same size and proportion of the boat that Ludo's brother had used whilst staying on Margaritari. *Why didn't I insist on providing him with a bigger and sturdier vessel? If I had it would have had a much better chance of staying afloat in those gusting winds than the one Theo used...the one Theo drowned beneath...*

But even as his heart pounded with renewed sorrow and regret Ludo couldn't help remembering his big brother's amused voice saying, 'You need more than one sailor to handle a bigger boat, little brother, and I want to be by myself on this holiday. I'm surrounded by people every working day of my life, and often during the night too if I'm on call. A small boat will do me just fine!'

Rubbing his chest with the heel of his hand, Ludo freed a heartfelt sigh. Some way, somehow, he was going to have to come to terms with what had happened to his brother properly, or the crowd of 'what ifs' and 'if onlys' would burden him for the rest of his life. He couldn't let that happen. If he did, then Theo's inspirational and admirable example of how to live a good and useful life would be buried along with his memory.

Once again he sought to divert his troubling thoughts with the memory of the honeyed heat of Natalie's sexy mouth and the feel of her slim, shapely body in his arms. Allowing himself a brief smile of anticipation, he wondered if tonight would be the night when she paid that visit to his room. The hope that she would made him realise that it had been at least an hour since he'd left her to her own devices—ostensibly to unpack and maybe to take a reviving shower after their travels, like he had. Surely she must be finished by now?

He'd noted that all she'd brought with her was one small suitcase and a tote. Women in Ludo's experience usually brought far more than that when going on holiday with him—but then he already intuitively knew that Natalie was unlike most of the women he was acquainted with. She was neither self-centred nor vain, and if he was right she wasn't trying to impress anybody either.

When he knocked on her door a couple of times and she didn't appear, he immediately turned on his heel and hurried downstairs to see where she had got to.

CHAPTER SEVEN

WITH HER INSIDES churning at the prospect of facing Ludo again after he'd stormed from the room, Natalie made herself unpack and hang up her clothes. This wasn't the way she'd envisaged her stay in Greece starting out.

In the streamlined, beautifully accessorised marble bathroom she took a quick cooling shower and then, in a bid to lift her spirits, selected one of her favourite dresses to wear. It was a burnt orange halter-neck in a flatteringly soft fabric that trailed elegantly down to her feet, and she teamed it with some pretty Indian bangles and flat Roman-style sandals. With the timeless Mediterranean glinting in the sun behind her, wearing the dress helped her feel as though she really *was* on holiday…at least so long as she didn't think about Ludo being angry with her, or the myriad of potentially difficult connotations of agreeing to pose as his fiancée.

What had he meant by his declaration that by the time she came to leave the very idea would break her heart? It had sounded as though he was furious that she would dare to deny him *anything*. It had already occurred to Natalie that he was probably a man who used physical gratification as a way to soothe deep private pain. Having been denied his chosen way of gaining some relief, it wasn't hard to understand why he'd reacted so furiously. The death of his brother and his own self-imposed exile from his home had to be weighing heavily on him. But, whatever Ludo's meaning, Natalie had heard pain and longing in his voice and that alone already had the power to break her heart.

Turning into the cavernous arched hallway that led to the dining room, kitchen and the herb garden so lovingly attended by Allena and her husband, Ludo discovered exactly where his guest had gone. She was immersed in animated conversation with Christos, and he saw with a start of pleasure that she was wearing the most beautiful burnt orange-coloured gown. Her long hair was arranged in a loose fashion on the top of her head, so that a few silken tendrils drifted free to frame her face, and the halter-necked design of the dress revealed her long slim neck and slender shoulders. The flowing material was the perfect foil for her stunning womanly form.

As if intuiting his presence Natalie turned, and the rose-tinted blush that heated her cheeks rendered her pretty as a picture. Ludo's lips shaped a deliberately slow and appreciative smile. 'So this is where you are. And I see that you have dressed for dinner. You look as lovely as Aphrodite herself. Come…let me look at you.'

Catching hold of her hand, he made her pivot slowly so that he could study every facet of the gown and her lovely, lissom shape. Behind them, Christos discreetly made his way out into the garden with a knowing smile.

'You remind me of a beautiful water-nymph in that

dress,' he commented, the timbre of his voice turning unwittingly husky.

'Aren't they supposed to be graceful, ephemeral creatures?' Her luminous grey eyes teasingly sparkled. 'You can't be comparing me to one of those, surely? When I was a child my dad always told me I was about as graceful as an elephant with two left feet.'

'I'd ask you if he was blind but, having met him, I know that he isn't.'

'No…I suppose he was just being realistic.'

'And you have carried the belief that you are not graceful around with you since you were a child?'

'It was just playful family banter. It doesn't mean that he didn't love me.'

As Natalie once again managed to bewitch him with her beautiful smile and sparkling eyes Ludo impetuously drew her against him, suddenly needing to hold her so he could once more experience the pleasure of having her in his arms, her exquisite feminine curves pressed up close to his body. It seemed that every time he touched her, every time he so much as *glanced* at her, a fire spread throughout his blood that wouldn't easily be extinguished. At least not until he made her his. Then and only then, when she gazed up at him with the same fever of longing and lust that he now experienced, would he attest to feeling remotely satisfied.

'He should have told you every day how beautiful, how precious you were to him,' he murmured, brushing a gentle kiss to the side of her velvet-soft cheek.

'He might never have said those exact words,' Natalie demurred, 'but I knew he felt the sentiment behind them. I'd hate you to get the wrong impression about him. Honestly, behind his bluff, confident exterior is a man who cares deeply about his loved ones.'

Happy to stay right where he was, with his hands resting lightly on the gentle flare of her slender and yet pleasingly curvaceous hips, Ludo stared hungrily back into the soft grey eyes and thoughtfully reflected on her comment.

'I seem to remember when we first met you questioned whether you were a kind and devoted daughter. In my opinion, from what I've observed so far Natalie, you most definitely *are*. But I think you take on far too much responsibility for your father. Is it your fault that he acquired the destructive habits that resulted in him being forced to sell his business?'

'Of course it isn't.'

Frowning, Natalie abruptly stepped away, and Ludo couldn't help regretting the impulse that had made him mention her father's debts. But he honestly felt aggrieved on her behalf. It was one thing being a good son or daughter, but quite another feeling responsible for every mistake a parent made. He sighed, and then, because she looked so enchanting, immediately found a smile.

'Please don't believe I am telling you how to think or feel. I am only concerned that you do not regard yourself enough. Also, it has been a lifelong habit of mine to be frank, and I know my earlier display of temper must have upset you.'

Moving nearer, he gently curled one of the long loose tendrils of hair that glanced against her cheek behind her ear. At first her answering smile was tentative and uncertain. But then, like the sun emerging from behind a rain cloud, the warm curve of her lips became quite simply exquisite.

'I'm not upset. The tensions of any journey can make a person snappy and on edge. But I'd like to be frank too, Ludo. I'm a firm believer that a worry shared is a worry halved. I know that you're still grieving for your brother, and you're worried about facing your parents after not seeing them for so long, but might it help you to talk about your concerns with me? Whatever you say, I promise I would never betray a confidence. I'd just listen and hopefully give you some support.'

'Of course you would.' His expression was sombre. 'It's probably what you do for all the waifs and strays and wounded hearts that come your way, isn't it? The bed and breakfast that you run with your mother is probably like a local, more comfortable branch of the Samaritans.' His lips twisted for a moment. 'And who wouldn't welcome a vision like you to talk to?'

He didn't mean to be cruel, but he couldn't quell the bitterness that suddenly surfaced in him. Why couldn't there have been someone like Natalie around when he'd heard the news that Theo had died? Someone he would have felt safe breaking his heart in front of? Someone who wouldn't judge him or see a chance to advance themselves in some way by their association with him?

He shook his head. 'I'm sorry, Natalie. But now is not the time for me to bare my soul. I am not saying I've completely closed the door on the possibility, but just not right now.'

She treated him to another understanding smile, and for a few captivating moments Ludo allowed himself simply to bask in it, as though it were warm rain after a cold, dry spell.

'Anyway,' she said, 'Christos was telling me about your garden—that it's full of orange and lemon trees. Can I see it?'

'It will be my pleasure to show you the garden, *glykia mou.*'

Cupping her elbow, Ludo couldn't help the glow of pride that swept through him that Natalie should be interested in the garden. The beauty and bounty of nature had always been one of his passions, right from when he was a boy, but apart from his mother, who had often talked about the healing power of it, he had rarely encountered women who felt the same way as he did.

Outside, Christos touched the tip of his straw hat in acknowledgement as Ludo and Natalie appeared. Speaking in Greek, he commented, 'You came at the right time to enjoy the oranges and lemons, Mr Petrakis. If you had left it much later the fruit would not have been at its best.'

'I know. And, by the way, thank you for all your hard work tending the gardens, Christos. I am convinced it is your magic touch that makes everything grow so abundantly.'

'It is my pleasure to be of service.'

Ludo was gratified to know that his devoted and respected employee was still happy to be working for him. When Christos and his wife retired he would make sure to provide them with a lovely home and garden so that he could continue enjoying his craft. Moving on, still cupping Natalie's elbow, Ludo guided her onto the meandering red stone path that led to the verdant green where the trees and fruit flourished so abundantly. Even before the trees came into view the air was drenched with the intoxicating scent of ripened fruit.

Breaking away from him, the woman by his side enthusiastically clapped her hands. 'This scent is incredible!' Her bright shining eyes and joyful enthusiasm were so engaging that for a moment Ludo was struck dumb.

'Walk on,' he invited smilingly, 'and you will see the fruit that is responsible.'

It was like walking into the Garden of Eden. Both the perfume and the sight of lush oranges and lemons hanging heavily from slim branches amid a bejewelled floral carpet of emerald-green was nothing less than wondrous. What added to her wonderment and pleasure was that her handsome companion seemed so much more relaxed than he had been earlier. It had given her heart when he'd told her he hadn't completely closed the door on baring his soul to her. A passing warm breeze lifted the gold lock of hair that glanced against his forehead, and in that instant he suddenly looked so carefree and young that she could imagine him in a gentler time, long before the unbearable tragedy of losing his beloved brother and separation from his homeland had etched indelible scars on his heart that likely would never be erased.

'It takes my breath away.' Shaking her head, she spontaneously held the palm of her hand over her heart.

'It makes me wonder what on earth I could have done to deserve being treated to such a sight.'

Without comment, Ludo walked over and took her by the hand. Unsure of what he was going to do, Natalie felt her heart drum hard as he led her across the grass to a fulsome lemon tree, plucked a plump yellow fruit from one of the branches, then tugged her hand towards him.

'Open your palm,' he instructed.

She obeyed, and he gave the lemon a hard squeeze so that the skin split and ripe juice spilled out into her hand like sparkling nectar, filling her nostrils with the sharp fresh scent of the sun-kissed fruit. As Ludo took his hand away Natalie moved her hand back and forth beneath her nose. 'It's glorious!' She smiled. 'It must be the freshest scent in the world.'

'If you add a teaspoon of sugar to the juice and rub your hands together I'm assured you'll have the best method of softening your skin that you could find.'

'How do you know that?'

With his sky-blue eyes squinting against the sunlight, Ludo grinned with pleasure.

'I heard about it from my mother. I used to watch her apply lemon juice and sugar to her hands after she'd washed the dishes. All I can tell you is that her hands were always soft as a child's. Don't take my word for it. When you get the chance give it a try.'

'I will.'

'Now, let's go over to the fountain and you can rinse your hands.'

At a magnificent solid-stone fountain, with its crystal-clear waters gushing from the upturned sculpted jug of a young shepherdess, Natalie rinsed her hands, bringing them up to her face to cool her sun-kissed cheeks. She knew it wasn't just the sun that had warmed them. Ludo Petrakis had cast the most mesmerising spell over her. A spell that right then she had no desire to ever be free of… 'That's better.' She smiled.

'Then I think we should go in to eat. Allena has prepared us something special, and if my guess is right it will probably be my favourite *moussaka,* followed by some *baklava.* I hope you have a sweet tooth, Natalie?'

'I do have a sweet tooth, and *baklava* happens to be a favourite of mine.'

Ludo's glance was slow and assessing, and in the ensuing momentary silence Natalie almost held her breath, wondering what he was thinking. She soon found out.

'It is very gratifying to know that you can yield to temptation, *glykia mou,*' he drawled. 'Because right now the temptation of *you* is sorely testing me.'

When he reached for her hand once again she let him clasp it without hesitation, loving the reassuring warmth of his touch and realising she could very easily become addicted to it.

Turning, Ludo led her back down the stone path and into the house…

After enjoying the superb moussaka and fresh three-bean salad that Allena had served them, also the delicious syrup-drenched baklava, they took their coffee out onto the terrace, where Ludo had first taken Natalie on their arrival. It was now almost full dusk, and the glass-like surface of the Mediterranean gleamed not with sunlight but with the bewitching, serene light of the moon.

Natalie leaned back in her rattan chair and sighed contentedly. About to share her thoughts on the beautiful scene with her companion, she saw that his eyelids were closed, and didn't know if he'd fallen into a light doze or was simply lost in thought. The journey on the plane had certainly been fraught with tension for him, knowing he was going back home for the first time since his brother's funeral. For now, she decided to keep her thoughts to herself so as not to disturb him.

It was certainly no hardship to relax with all the breathtaking beauty on display, and Natalie couldn't help but include Ludo in that description. More and more she was starting to believe that he was right. It *would* break her heart to leave this place…to leave *him*. The thought made her sit up with a jolt. The impulse she'd followed in accepting his deal to come with him was dangerously beginning to backfire on her. And tomorrow he was going to introduce her to his parents as his *fiancée*. As much as she was enamoured of this wonderful country, and longed to have the time to explore some of it, Natalie wondered if she really could go through with the pretence Ludo had suggested after all.

The sudden unexpected movement of his hand over a hard-muscled thigh in his cream-coloured chinos alerted her to the fact that he wasn't dozing at all, but just sitting quietly.

Reaching forward to collect her cup of coffee from the table, she ventured, 'Ludo? Are you all right?'

'Of course I'm all right. Why do you ask?'

'I was just concerned about how you were feeling. Ever since I told you that my mum had heard about what happened to your brother I've had the sense you've been retreating little by little. You hardly talked at all on the journey here. I didn't mean to upset you by telling you what she said.'

Lifting his hand to his forehead, Ludo rubbed a little, his blue eyes glinting warily as a cat's when confronted by some potential sudden danger.

'I sometimes think that Greek people round the world have an uncanny sense of knowing what's going on with each other even if they've never met. I shouldn't have been surprised that your mother had heard of the tragedy, but I was. If I seem to have shut down a little it's because any reference to my brother inevitably brings back great sadness and regret for me. I am also going to have to face my parents tomorrow and explain to them why I ran away after the funeral.'

Natalie swallowed hard. 'Ran away?'

'Yes. I packed my bags and left straight after the funeral without giving them any real explanation. I couldn't deal with their grief. It cut me like a knife to see them so heartbroken…not knowing what to do anymore. They had always been just like my brother Theo—steady and dependable. As if nothing, not even an earthquake, could shake their unified solidity.' He shook his head, agitatedly combing his fingers through his golden sun-streaked hair. 'And instead of supporting them through that terrible time and providing solace I chose to escape. I wanted to try and blot out the past and all that had happened by losing myself in my work and trying my damndest not to think about it.'

'And did that help?'

'Of course it didn't help!' Furious with himself, with Natalie, and perhaps with the whole world too, Ludo shot up from his chair, breathing hard. 'I discovered you can run away as far as you like—even to the remotest place on the planet—but you can't leave your sorrow and grief behind. Wherever you go, the pain travels with you. All running away did for me was add to my already unbearable sense of guilt and inadequacy. The realisation that as a son I had totally failed my parents— the people I love the most. They devoted their lives to raising me and Theo and look how I repaid them. It's unforgivable.'

The anguish in his voice immediately made Natalie get to her feet. 'You didn't do it deliberately, Ludo. It wasn't planned. You were hurting too, remember? It was a totally understandable reaction.'

Dropping his hands to his lean straight hips, he trapped her gaze with the sheer desolation in his eyes. 'The only way I can make it up to them is by introducing you as my fiancée, Natalie. That's why you have to do this for me. It is not enough that I return home by myself.'

'Why?' She stepped round the table to face him. 'Why isn't it enough? You're their beloved son, Ludo. A son any parents would be proud of. And people forgive those they love. Even when they've done the so-called "unforgivable".'

'Do they indeed?' His burning blue eyes gleamed

cynically. 'I wonder how you have become such an optimist. It is my experience that forgiving someone who has hurt you, and hurt you badly, is the hardest thing of all.'

'But if you see that you only hurt yourself more by not forgiving them, then maybe it's not so hard. For instance, when my dad walked out on my mum and me, I felt so heartbroken and betrayed that I thought I'd never trust him again. How could he do such a thing to us? I thought he was a liar and a cheat and deserved never to be happy again! For a long time I didn't even want to see him. But through it all my mum wouldn't hear one bad word said about him and she urged me to forgive him. Trust me, it wasn't easy... But it had to be done if I was ever to have any peace, because it was killing me holding all that blame and hurt in my heart. Then, when he had his heart attack, the decision to forgive him for everything was easy. I'm so glad I realised it, because now our relationship is closer than ever.'

Her heart was galloping as she came to the end of her impassioned speech—a speech that had asserted feelings she hadn't expressed to anyone before. Not even her mum.

Combing her fingers shakily through her hair, Natalie was appalled at herself. 'I'm sorry' she murmured, 'We were talking about your parents. I only wanted to illustrate that I believe if you really love someone that love never dies. I don't doubt for one second that your parents have already forgiven you, Ludo. My mother once told me that the love for your child surpasses any other and lives on even when a parent dies.'

Now her face was burning. The man in front of her had neither moved nor tried to interrupt her. Instead, the long, considered glance he was giving her suggested he was thinking hard, hopefully finding some solace in her assertion that a parent's love never died, no matter what their offspring had done. Natalie could only pray that it was true.

Beneath the white linen shirt he was wearing Ludo's broad athletic shoulders lifted in an enigmatic shrug that revealed very little about what he felt, and her anxiety skyrocketed—she had blundered in where maybe she shouldn't have.

'Whether my parents forgive me or not, we will find out tomorrow. But right now I intend to go for a very long walk so I can reflect on our reunion.'

'Would you like me to go with you?'

One corner of his mouth lifted slightly towards a high bronzed cheekbone. 'No. This is one walk that I must take on my own. If you want some entertainment ask Allena to show you what we have available. And if you think of anything else you need, just ask her. If you feel that you want an early night, go ahead. Don't trouble to wait up for me. We can talk again in the morning over breakfast. *Kalinihta,* Natalie. Sleep well.'

Stepping closer, Ludo almost absentmindedly brushed her cheek with his warm lips, and as he turned and walked away the warmth from his body stirred the air, mingling with the scent of bougainvillaea draped heavily over the terrace walls, as if the flowers too registered his leaving and couldn't help but be saddened by it.

CHAPTER EIGHT

HE LIKED THE night. Even more, he liked the night air of his country. No matter where a person went on the island, they breathed in air that was drenched with an eclectic variety of sensual aromas. Some of the most pervading scents were of olives and pine, bougainvillaea and jasmine, crusty bread baked in traditional fire ovens. And wherever people ate the delicious aroma of roasted meats and the freshest fish imaginable would tempt even the most jaded of appetites. But more than the tempting food and scents that lured tourists to the country time and time again Ludo loved the sight and sound of the Mediterranean and the Aegean best of all. It had always calmed and centred him, no matter what worry might be plaguing him at the time.

But the day he'd heard that Theo had drowned in the waters off Margaritari was the day that Ludo had come to *despise* the sea. How could he ever take pleasure in it again after it had so cruelly taken his brother from him?

Walking along the near deserted beach, he stopped to gaze up at the bewitching crescent moon that hung in the inky dome above him.

'Make a wish on the crescent moon,' his mother had

often told him and his brother when they were boys. 'If you do, it is bound to come true, my children.'

Well, Ludo had wished to be as rich as Croesus. No doubt Theo had made a much more humanitarian plea to be of service to those less fortunate than himself. Even as a young boy he had exhibited uncommon kindness and patience. But, no matter how wealthy or powerful he became, Ludo knew he would instantly give up every single euro he had if he could have his brother back.

Once again, a familiar arrow of grief pierced him as though he were on fire and, rubbing his chest in a bid to try and ease the pain, he made himself walk farther on down the beach. One or two tourists greeted him, and after reluctantly acknowledging them he quickly moved on. He wasn't in the mood to be sociable tonight.

Having removed his canvas shoes as soon as he'd stepped onto the sand, and despite the sorrow and regret that weighed him down, he briefly luxuriated in the sensation of sun-baked golden grains on the soles of his feet. The thought came to him that he should have brought Natalie. Why had he turned down her offer to accompany him? He should know by now that her presence soothed him. Soothed him and *aroused* him.

He suddenly felt a strong urge to hear her voice, to listen to the encouraging advice that seemed to come to her so naturally. What if he let down his guard and admitted he no longer wanted to endure the fears and concerns that plagued him on his own? What if he asked Natalie to *share* them? Would she be willing to do that for him?

But even as he mulled the idea over in his head Ludo

remembered how she had urged him to believe that his parents had already forgiven him for his negligence. It had dangerously raised hopes that would be cruelly dashed if they had not. Then where would he be? His so-called success meant nothing if he didn't have their unconditional love and respect.

His thoughts returned to Natalie. Would she have taken up his suggestion and had an early night? During their meal that evening she'd shielded a yawn from him more than once. She was probably looking forward to a good night's sleep—while he undoubtedly faced another torturous night wrestling with his fears about how tomorrow would go.

Damn it all to hell! Why couldn't he have engineered a simpler existence than the one he'd chosen? Instead of obsessively working himself into the ground and trying to accumulate even more wealth, what he wouldn't give right now to be wooing the love of his life—as his father had done when he'd met his mother—to be anticipating building a home and family together and perhaps living a good part of the year on Margaritari as he'd once dreamed he would? It hit him how tired he'd grown of the endless travelling that filled most of his year. What he really wanted to do was to spend some proper time with family and friends, to immerse himself again in the simple but solid values that shone like a beacon of goodness and common sense in a world that frequently moved too fast, where people restlessly went from one meaningless pleasure to the next in search of that most elusive goal of all…*happiness*.

The truth was that, for Ludo, the dog-eat-dog busi-

ness world that he'd so eagerly embraced had all but
lost its appeal since Theo died. He might have sought
refuge in it when he'd exiled himself from his parents,
but the exercise had failed miserably. All it had shown
him was how emotionally barren his life had become.
He was just kidding himself that he wanted to keep on
travelling down the same soulless path. In truth, Ludo
had missed his home and country much more than he'd
realised.

Unbidden, a mental vision stole into his mind of Natalie holding out her hand beneath the lemon tree, so that
Ludo might demonstrate the ripeness of the fruit. There
was a strangely alluring innocence about her that grew
more and more compelling every time he saw her. But it
was playing merry havoc with his libido. Just thinking
about her graceful slender figure, her river of shining
hair and big grey eyes, made him feel near *desperate* to
take her between his sheets and passionately seduce her.

Would she ever feel inclined, or indeed brave enough,
to invite herself into his room one of these nights, as
he'd suggested? Ludo didn't know why, but despite their
almost instantaneous connection he'd intuited that he
shouldn't seduce Natalie just to fulfil his own hungry
desire for gratification. He should give her time to realise that her own needs were just as great as his. When
she came round to the fact of her own free will, the heat
between them would be nothing less than *explosive,* he
was sure.

But it didn't help to dwell on the tantalising prospect. Kicking at the sand with another frustrated sigh,
he found himself ambling towards the seashore.

He wasn't the only one to be won over by Natalie's charms. During dinner her genteel manners and ready smile had clearly formed a bond between her and Allena. Given the opportunity, would a similar bond ever be forged between Natalie and his own mother? Irritably reminding himself that their engagement was nothing but a bittersweet ruse, born of a desire to convince his parents to see him in a better light, Ludo emitted a furious curse. Reaching down, he picked up a small jagged rock that was half buried beneath the sand and threw it into the foaming moonlit waves lapping onto the shore.

Natalie had been so tired that she'd fallen asleep on the bed fully dressed. She'd tried hard to wait up for Ludo, but when the evening had worn on and he still hadn't shown she'd regretfully made her way upstairs to the bedroom.

After staring out at the moonlit sea from the terrace for what seemed like an eternity, thinking how tragic it was that the revered and beloved Theo had perished there beneath the waves, she'd found herself overwhelmed by a sense of sadness she hadn't been able to dispel easily. Lost in her poignant daydream, she'd experienced a moment of real panic, imagining Ludo walking alone by the seashore, with nothing but sorrow and regret accompanying him. She should have insisted that she join him, even if he'd got angry. It would have been worth the risk to make sure he was all right.

Finally, unable to fight what felt like sheer exhaustion, Natalie had crossed the room to the lavish bed, sat down to remove her sandals and before she knew it, had lain down curled up in a foetal position and fallen fast asleep.

She didn't have a clue what time it was when she woke the next morning, but the sun beaming in through the open patio doors was glorious. When she sat up and saw that she still wore the pretty orange dress she'd had on last night she shook her head in disbelief. That had never happened before. But then yesterday had been full-on, with all the travelling and its accompanying tension—that tension increasing when Ludo had chosen to go for a moonlit walk on his own last night and she hadn't seen him return.

Hurriedly stripping off the colourful dress, Natalie headed straight into the bathroom. But not before nervously wondering if Ludo thought her ungracious or rude for not waiting up for him. After all, it was hardly the behaviour of the supposedly devoted fiancée his parents were expecting to meet today, was it? The realisation of what she had pledged to do hit her again like a head-on collision. But the shock that eddied through her also acted as a spur for her to hurry up and present herself to her host. She realised she had a lot of questions to ask about their proposed visit to his family home.

A smiling Allena informed Natalie that Ludo was out on the terrace, waiting for her to join him for breakfast. Drawing in a long, deep breath, she hovered in an arched doorway that was draped with blossom, silently observing him as he lounged in a cane chair with his knees drawn up against his chest and his arms loosely wrapped round them.

His attire today consisted of a casual white linen shirt and rust-coloured chinos. His feet were bare. With the stunning vista of the sparkling ocean glinting in the sun before him, his sun-kissed golden hair and long limbs made him resemble a beautiful dancer in repose, and her heartbeat skittered nervously. She was utterly mesmerised by the breathtaking picture he made.

Turning suddenly, he took her completely by surprise with his greeting. How long had he known she was standing there?

'*Kalimera,* Natalie. I trust you slept well?' he drawled, smiling.

The stunning sapphire eyes that crinkled at the corners when he utilised his smile rendered her temporarily speechless.

Quickly gathering her wits, she replied, 'I slept like a log, thanks. In fact I was so tired last night that I fell asleep fully clothed and didn't wake up until about half an hour ago. I hope I haven't kept you waiting too long?'

'I was expecting you to arrive at any moment—so, no. You didn't keep me waiting too long. And even if you did it was worth the wait. You look very lovely in that dress.'

The simply-cut cornflower-blue dress that Natalie wore had short sleeves and a pretty sweetheart neckline, embroidered with the tiniest of white daisies, and the folds of the skirt draped softly down to her knees. She loved it because her mother had bought it for her trip to Greece, professing it to be modestly respectable but pretty enough to win her the 'right' kind of attention. There was only one man whose attention she wanted to win, Natalie privately acknowledged, and that was the real-life Adonis sitting in front of her.

'Thanks. My mum bought it for me.'

'Ahh… Now I see why you chose to wear it today. It's exactly the kind of dress that a Greek mother would buy for her young and beautiful daughter. A dress she can confidently wear to a family gathering with friends and relations. It is suitably virginal and will definitely make the right impression,' he teased. 'Now, why don't you come to the table and help yourself to some yogurt and honey for breakfast?'

Still reeling from his comment that her dress was 'suitably virginal', Natalie hurriedly pulled out a chair opposite him and sat down—anything to stop Ludo seeing that she was blushing painfully. As she scooped some yogurt into a cereal bowl from the generous ceramic dish in front of her she was in no hurry to meet his omniscient gaze.

'I waited up for you for quite some time last night,' she told him. 'What time did you get in?'

'About one or two in the morning.' He shrugged. 'Who knows? I was hardly keeping track of the time.'

'Did it help to clear your head, going for such a long walk?'

'Perhaps.' His reply was painfully non-committal.

'It's a tremendously brave thing that you're doing, Ludo—coming back home after three years and facing what happened,' she told him encouragingly. 'Your parents must be so happy at the prospect of seeing you again.'

'You are an eternal optimist, I think.'

'Maybe I am.' Natalie frowned. 'But I'd rather believe in hope and resolution than be cynical.'

'You should try some honey with your yogurt. I am sure you know it is traditional.'

Suddenly his piercing blue eyes were boring into hers and she forgot what she'd been going to say.

'Here...'

Leaning towards her, he scooped up a teaspoon of the richly golden nectar. Just when Natalie expected him to stir it into her helping of yogurt he touched the spoon to her lips for her to sample it instead. Her body tightened and the tips of her breasts tingled fiercely at the sensual nature of the gesture. Obediently and self-consciously she licked the honey off the spoon. The whole time she was hotly aware that Ludo was staring at her.

'Hmm,' she responded, emitting a soft sigh. 'It's delicious.'

Her expression was no longer self-conscious but laced with helpless invitation. The man was driving her crazy! Natalie might not be experienced in the art of seduction, but she was getting close to desperate for Ludo to seduce *her*. In turn, he gave her an amused slow smile that made her want to rip off his shirt, discard the pretty blue dress that he'd declared 'suitably virginal' and all but drag him across the table and insist he make love to her...

The thought made her bite her lip to prevent herself from giggling because it was so outrageous. It was also diametrically opposed to anything she'd ever contemplated in her life before.

'You're such a goody-two-shoes when it comes to

men, Nat,' a friend had once teased her. 'Haven't you ever met a man you simply just *had* to have?'

Not until she'd set eyes on Ludo Petrakis, she hadn't...

'You looked like you were about to laugh. What was so funny?' Ludo asked, depositing the spoon he'd used for the honey on a saucer.

'A crazy thought came into my mind, that's all,' she admitted warily.

'Want to share it with me?'

'No.' Tucking her hair behind her ear, she shrugged carelessly in a bid to deflect his curiosity. 'At least not right now. Can you tell me a little bit more about your parents before I meet them? And is it possible to stop off somewhere on the way to buy your mother a gift? I'd really like to get her something. Does she like flowers?'

'Of course—but she has a large garden full of flowers. You don't have to worry about getting her a gift. Your presence as my fiancée will be gift enough, Natalie.'

Feeling suddenly deflated, she frowned. Her brow puckered. 'But I'm not your fiancée, am I? We're only pretending that I am.'

The muscle that flinched in the side of his smooth tanned cheekbone indicated his annoyance. 'I know that.'

'At any rate, it's polite to take a gift when someone invites you into their home for the first time, isn't it?'

He sighed. 'If it means that much to you, angel, then we will stop off at a place I know and purchase a nice vase that she might put her own flowers in. Will that suffice?'

Feeling marginally better, Natalie somehow found a smile. 'Thank you. It does. Will you tell me a bit about what your mother is like? I'd really like to know.'

Ludo's expression instantly relaxed, as though the topic couldn't help but fill him with pleasure.

'She is a beautiful woman and a wonderful mother and she loves to put people at ease when they visit her. What else can I tell you?' His blue eyes twinkled in amusement. 'She is an incredible cook and an accomplished seamstress—she was a dressmaker before she met my father. He utterly relies on her, you know? But he wouldn't thank me for telling you that. He is a typical "man's man" and proud of it. Now, can you do something for me before we talk further?'

'What would that be?'

Her heart jumped a mile high as her gaze fell into his dazzling blue irises. She was still aroused. It was surely an impossible challenge to hold his glance for long and not reveal her desire? With his elbows resting on the table, Ludo leaned in a little closer—so close that she could count every single long golden lash that fringed his eyelids.

'Can you try not to look so adorable when you smile?' he asked huskily. 'It makes me want to wipe the smile clean off your face with a hot, languorous kiss that would very likely lead me into removing that pretty virginal dress your mother bought you and more besides.'

Just in time Natalie suppressed a groan. 'I don't think—I mean, I think we should—we should—'

'Give it a try?'

Swallowing hard, she reached for a white paper napkin and touched it to her lips, lightly dabbing at them. 'I think we should stay on a safer subject, don't you?'

'Even if it's nearly killing me to have you look at me with those innocent grey eyes and not tell you in graphic detail what I'd like us to do together in bed?'

'That's how I make you feel?' Her voice had dropped to a shocked whisper.

'You have no idea,' he growled, then abruptly got to his feet and drove his long fingers through his hair. 'But no doubt it will keep. We have to make the journey to see my parents very soon, and I suppose we should concentrate on getting ready.'

'How long will it take us to get there?'

'About an hour.'

'Where exactly do they live?'

'About four kilometres from Lindos, but the area is quite rural in comparison to the town. Thankfully, it's also close to the beach.'

'And that's where you grew up?'

Once again Natalie registered wariness in Ludo's eyes. He was still apprehensive about seeing his parents, and probably fearing the worst about their reception of him. She wished she knew a way to help put him more at ease.

He turned away to gaze out at the sea. 'Yes…it is where my brother Theo and I grew up. We had a truly magical childhood, living there. We were so free— which should be the right of all children, in my view. Most days we ran down to the beach to play before school. Then we'd run home in anticipation of our breakfast.'

'You had breakfast? I know that many Greeks don't… apart from drinking coffee, I mean.'

'My mother believed it was important for children to start the day with some food in their bellies.' With a wryly arched brow, he turned back towards her. 'She gave us soft cheese spread on sesame-seeded *psomi* to eat.'

'I love that bread. My mum still makes it now and then, especially when we have friends to dinner.'

Joining him, Natalie was mindful of not disturbing his poignant and unexpectedly heart-warming train of thought and couldn't deny the warmth it instigated in her own heart that he would share the memory with her.

'You will have to tell my mother. She is sure to want to know all about it.' Lifting his palm, Ludo briefly pressed it to her cheek, as if he didn't trust himself to let it linger. 'I think it's time that we went. If there is anything else you wish to ask me you can ask it on the journey.'

In the next instant he'd moved swiftly away to the open patio doors, and before she could reply he disappeared inside.

CHAPTER NINE

THE TRADITIONALLY BUILT white house that was so familiar to Ludo loomed up before them minutes before the Range Rover reached the end of the rutted undulating track they'd been travelling on. Although the architecture was typical of many homes in the locale, it was unusually tall and imposing. Built on the crest of a hill, it could be seen for miles.

The unmade track was very soon replaced by a smooth driveway lined with fig trees that led directly to the house's white-stone arched terrace. Behind the dwelling the deceptively calm waters of the Aegean created the most stunning iridescent backdrop, and even though he knew the house and the view well, it still made Ludo draw breath at the beauty of it.

But he didn't contemplate the scene for very long. Parking the car, he felt his stomach churn at the prospect of his first encounter with his parents after three long years. Was it possible that they would ever forgive him for his desertion at a time when they'd most needed him…particularly his mother? If they didn't, then he would simply just have to wish them well and walk away again—even if it broke his heart.

'Ludo?'

Beside him, Natalie's soft voice halted his painful reflection, reminding him he wasn't going to have to do this on his own. He remembered thinking about the possibility of sharing his worries with her last night and the tension in the pit of his belly eased a little.

'It's going to be all right.'

She smiled, and he reached out for her small hand and squeezed it in gratitude. It struck him afresh how pretty and innocent she looked today in the simple blue dress her mother had bought her. The conservative sweetheart neckline revealed not the slightest décolletage, yet in his opinion a sexy black cocktail dress couldn't have been nearly as alluring or beguiling.

'I'm sure you are right. If anyone has the ability to convince me of that it is you, *agapiti mou*. Let's do this, shall we?' His voice was gruffer than he'd meant it to be, but the relinquishing of his guard had left him feeling curiously vulnerable.

As he stepped down from the Range Rover onto the patterned marble drive he glanced towards the entrance of the house. With his heart beating double time he saw his parents walking towards them. Wearing an elegant blue tunic over white palazzo pants, her dark blonde hair shorter than he'd seen her wear it before, his mother Eva looked as effortlessly elegant as ever, if a little thinner. She was holding on to his father's strong muscled arm.

Unusually, his father was wearing a suit, as if to instigate some formality into the proceedings and perhaps to remind his errant son that he was a long way from being forgiven and accepted…at least by *him*.

Acutely aware that emotions were probably running high in all of them, Ludo returned his gaze to his mother and saw her smile tentatively, as if unsure how he was going to receive her. That uncertain look on her beautiful face twisted his heart. Yet because his father's expression was so serious he hesitated to throw his arms round her as he longed to.

He needn't have worried. Releasing her husband's arm, Eva Petrakis stepped onto the mosaic tiles where Ludo stood and wholeheartedly embraced him. Her still slender body trembled as he hugged her back without hesitation, his senses awash in a sea of childhood memories of her unstinting love and affection for him and his brother. Oh, how he had missed her!

With her hands resting lightly but firmly on his arms, as if she was reluctant to let him go, she stood back to scan his features. In Greek, she told him how worried she'd been about him, and that every night when she went to bed she'd prayed he was safe and well and planning on coming home soon...home where he belonged.

In return, Ludo murmured his sincere apology and regret. She smiled, gently touching his face. Then she told him that she knew far more of how he felt than he'd realised. There was no need for him ever to feel sorry about his actions again. She understood and had never blamed him for them, so neither should he blame himself. As hard as it had been for her and Alekos to accept, they had now reconciled themselves to the fact that it had been Theo's time. It was their profound belief that he was home with God now...

Leaning towards him, she planted a warmly affectionate kiss on Ludo's cheek and, lowering her voice, told him that he should give his father a little more time to realise what a great gift it was for them to have him home again. 'Be patient,' she advised sagely.

Observing his father across her shoulder, Ludo saw that sorrow and time had indeed taken their toll on him. There were deep grooves in the forehead of his handsome face, and his curling dark hair was more liberally sprinkled with salt and pepper strands than it had been three years ago. But without a doubt he still emitted the same formidable energy that Theo had envied so much.

'If I live to be my father's age and still have the strength and energy to accomplish as much in one day as he can,' he'd often declared, 'then I'll know the Petrakis gene pool hasn't failed me!'

Swallowing down the lump that swelled in his throat at the bittersweet memory, Ludo moved away from his mother and determinedly went to stand in front of the man who had been responsible for raising him.

'Hello, Father,' he greeted him. 'It has been too long, yes?'

Even though he was absolutely sincere—because events and the passage of time had rendered the already considerable distance between them a veritable chasm—his words couldn't help but sound awkward and strained. Instead of embracing the older man, as he might normally have done, he held out his hand. Alekos Petrakis didn't take it. Ludo's tentative hopes for a reconciliation splintered like shattered glass.

'So you have deigned to come home at long last?' his father remarked coldly. 'I had hoped you would grow into a man to equal your brother Theo in conduct and character, but your absence these past three years has demonstrated to me that I hoped in vain. I do not recognise you, Ludovic, and it grieves me sorely that I do not.'

Ludo reeled. It felt as though he'd been punched hard. 'I am sorry you feel like that, Father. But Theo has his path and I have mine.'

The shame-filled break in his voice catapulted him back to being the small boy who'd longed to have his father regard him as highly as he did his big brother, and he couldn't help flinching in embarrassment as well as pain. The older man's admission had all but floored him. Didn't he see *any* good in him at all? Were the only people who had any kind of belief in his worth the two women who stood patiently waiting for him to join them?

'Had,' his father corrected him. 'You said Theo "has" his path. Your brother is no longer with us, remember?'

Ludo silently cursed the unfortunate blunder. The accusing look in his father's brown eyes cut him to the quick. Hardly able to bear it, he turned away, seeing with a jolt of surprise that his mother Eva had moved up close to Natalie and was exchanging a reassuring smile with her. Natalie held out the slim glass vase she had insisted on buying as a gift and his mother graciously accepted it. Remembering that she'd advised him to be patient with regard to his father, he determinedly quashed any further thoughts of failure and remorse and returned to the women.

'He doesn't want to know me,' he murmured, glancing ruefully at his mother, then at Natalie.

'He just needs a little more time, my son,' she answered in English. 'You both do. Time to get to know each other again.' Carefully setting down the delicate vase on a wrought-iron table behind them, Eva reached for his hand and gently squeezed it. 'Now, we have all been dreadfully remiss. You have not introduced us to your beautiful fiancée, Ludo, and I'd like you to remedy that. She has just given me the most beautiful vase as a gift and I am taken aback by her generosity.'

Without hesitation Ludo caught hold of Natalie's hand and gripped it firmly. An instantaneous bolt of electricity flashed between them and for a long moment his glance cleaved to hers. He wished they were somewhere more private, so he could show her *exactly* how she made him feel. It was a revelation that he seemed to need her so much. At the same time he knew it was important to make the proper introductions.

'Mother, this is Natalie Carr—and Natalie…this is my mother, Eva Petrakis.'

'*Kalos orises,* Natalie. Although I'm told that you are half-Greek, I will speak to you in English because my son tells me you do not speak Greek at home with your mother. It is a shame you do not speak it, but I'm sure that will change given time. I cannot tell you how long I have waited for the moment when I would welcome my soon-to-be daughter to our home, and it comes as no surprise to me to find that you are so beautiful. My son has always had the most exquisite taste.'

Natalie found herself affectionately hugged by the elegant and friendly Eva in a waft of classic Arpège perfume. She smiled because it was the same fragrance that her mother wore, and it made her feel immediately at home.

'*Yia sas.*' Using one of the few greetings in Greek she *did* know, she said hello. 'It's so nice to meet you, Mrs Petrakis. Ludo always talks about you with such affection.'

She stole a glance at the man standing silently by her side, quite aware that he'd become even more uneasy since that short conversation just now with his father. The older man seemed formidably stern to her. She would dearly love to know what had transpired between them, and guessed it wasn't good.

His mother, on the other hand, was clearly a different proposition. She seemed much more forgiving and approachable. And even though Natalie wasn't really the 'soon-to-be daughter' she'd longed for, strangely she wasn't embarrassed that it wasn't the truth. All she could think right then was that Ludo needed her help. More than that, she'd made a contract with him that she was bound to follow through on. He'd kept his part of the bargain by giving her father a better deal for his business, and now she had to act the part of his fiancée convincingly…at least until the time came for her to return to the UK.

The thought was a harsh and sobering one.

'Ludo has always been my baby.' Eva smiled, her gaze lovingly meeting her son's. 'He was always such a mischievous little boy, but I loved that he was so playful and liked to have fun. Our friends and neighbours adored him. They called him the golden-haired Petrakis angel.'

Beneath his lightly tanned chiselled features Ludo reddened a little. The realisation that his mother's tender little speech had embarrassed him made Natalie warm to him even more, because she guessed how much the fond declaration must secretly please him. After what had happened three years ago he must be all but *starving* for a demonstration of his parents' love and affection—along with their forgiveness.

'Come with me, Natalie.' Firmly grasping her hand, Eva started to walk Natalie over to the man who stood silently and a little broodingly, observing them all. 'I want to introduce you to my husband—Ludo's father—Alekos Petrakis.'

'*Yia sas.* It's a pleasure to meet you, Mr Petrakis.'

She tried hard to inject some confidence into her tone but it wasn't easy. Not when she had the distinct feeling that the man with the unflinchingly direct brown eyes was not an easy man to fool. But to Natalie's surprise he warmly captured her hand between his much larger palms and his pleased smile seemed utterly genuine.

'*Kalos orises,* Natalie. So you are the woman who is brave enough to take on my son Ludovic?'

Her heart thumped hard as she started to reply. 'You never know, Mr Petrakis—maybe Ludo is the brave one? We haven't known each other for very long. When he gets to know me a little better he might discover that I have a few unappealing traits that can't help but irritate him.'

To her surprise, Alekos threw back his leonine head and laughed heartily. But before he could make a comment, Ludo usurped him.

'I doubt that very much, my angel. You have too many traits that please me to counteract my being irritated by any less appealing ones. Plus, you are very easy on the eye…do you not agree, Father?'

Natalie hardly dared to breathe. What was clear to her was that Ludo was holding out an olive branch to his stern parent…trying to disperse some of the tension between them with light humour. She prayed his father would recognise that was what he intended. The older man gave a slight downward nod of his head to indicate yes, and the dark eyes flicked appreciatively over Natalie's face.

'Your wife-to-be is certainly bewitching.' He smiled, and Eva Petrakis' coral-painted mouth curved with a delighted smile of her own. Linking her arm with her husband's, she looked searchingly at Natalie and frowned. 'Why are you not wearing an engagement ring? Has my charming son not purchased one for you yet?'

Touching his hand to Natalie's back, Ludo let it slide downwards so that he could encircle her waist. His fingers firmed against her ribcage beneath her dress, and she couldn't deny that his warm touch helped her feel more secure.

'We were waiting until we arrived in Greece to select one.'

His dazzling blue eyes emitted a silent signal for her to agree with him.

'In fact I intend to call a jeweller friend of mine in Lindos about it tomorrow.'

'And I presume you have asked Natalie's father for

her hand in marriage?' Alekos challenged with a frown. 'You know it is the custom.'

Ludo pulled her closer into his side. Had he sensed her tremble just then? Suddenly their pretence at being engaged was presenting more problems than she'd anticipated. Out of the blue, Natalie recalled her mother's stories of her childhood in Crete. An engaged couple's parents also had to have a period of getting to know one another before their children were wed. Why hadn't she remembered that when she'd agreed with Ludo to masquerade as his fiancée? More importantly, why hadn't *he*?

'It all happened so suddenly...what we feel for each other, I mean.'

Incredibly, Ludo was gazing into her eyes as though he meant every word he was saying. Her heart galloped as hard as a racehorse out of the starting gates and her mouth turned dry as sand. It was as though she'd suddenly been plunged into some fantastical dream.

'We have barely had time to think about anything other than the fact we want to be together,' he explained. 'When we return to the UK I will be formally asking Natalie's father for her hand, just as soon as we can arrange a meeting.'

'And afterwards you must come back to us, so that we may have an engagement party for you. If Natalie's parents would like to be there—as I am sure they will—you must ring me straight away so that we can organise things, my son.' His mother's voice was both happy and eager. Her beaming glance fell on Natalie. 'I know it has all been rather sudden for you, my dear, but do you have any idea at all about a date for the wedding?'

'We were thinking that later on in the year might be better. Perhaps autumn,' Ludo interjected smoothly, robbing her of the chance to reply.

It was just as well, Natalie thought. She was far too stunned that he should be anywhere near mentioning a date when in reality they both knew that the event wasn't even going to take place. Just as soon as they were alone again they were going to have to have a very serious talk, because right now events were taking on all the urgency and speed of an ambulance crew racing hell for leather to an emergency, and she wasn't confident she could halt them.

The deceit was making her feel intensely uncomfortable…not to mention *guilty*. Yet despite her unease, Natalie felt a sense of heartfelt disappointment that she *wasn't* engaged to Ludo, wasn't going to marry him. The undeniable revelation that she was head over heels in love with him made it hard to project even the most temporary appearance of composure.

'So you are going to adhere to the traditional time for a marriage, when the olive harvest is gathered in?' Ludo's father was nodding his approval of the idea. 'I think that is a very wise choice. It will help people see that you are a man of principle, Ludovic…a man to whom family values are still important.'

He might almost have added *after all* to that statement, Natalie thought, tensing anxiously. The immediate sight of a muscle jerking in the side of Ludo's sculpted cheekbone told her he had read his father's declaration in the same way and vehemently resented it. In the next instant he confirmed it.

'So you do not believe I was a man who had principles and family values before, Father?' he ground out tersely.

Natalie's stomach plunged at the sudden potential for familial disaster.

'I speak as I find,' Alekos answered stiffly. 'If you ever indeed had both those qualities, then you clearly lost them when your brother died.'

With a furious curse Ludo spun away from Natalie to stand in front of his father. She flinched. His pain at being so cruelly judged by his own flesh and blood was agonisingly tangible.

'Why?' he demanded, glaring. 'Because you conclude I left without reason? Did you never ask yourself *why* I needed to put so much distance between us? Did you not guess how much I was hurting, too? When Theo died I would have given anything for the accident to have happened to *me,* not him! *He* was the one everyone regarded as a good man—a son to be proud of—and he was! He was amazing, and the work that he did was of benefit to hundreds...maybe thousands of families. Whereas I—'

Suddenly he was staring down at the ground, shaking his head in bewilderment and rage. 'I directed my talents to making money...a *lot* of money. It's almost like a dirty word to you, Father, isn't it? I'm not worthy enough to be thought of as good, even if I *can* help people by creating jobs. And you know what? I learned how to become rich from *you.* It takes blood, sweat and tears to make it in this world—you taught me that. Work hard and the world will be your oyster—then you can have anything you want. That was your mantra all through our childhood. But when Theo became a doctor you decided to make a distinction between what was good and what was bad. And you did it because you liked the kudos and admiration you got from your friends due to your son being a renowned doctor.'

Breathing hard, Ludo scraped his fingers through his hair. 'Well, I am what I am, and it hardly matters what you think of me now. But you should know that Theo was the best friend I could ever have wished for. He was my ally, too. I'll always remember him not just for being my brother but for the love and support he gave me throughout our time together. *He* was the wise man who told me it would only cause me more pain if I fought against your prejudice when you always made it clear that you preferred him to me. "Just be yourself," he told me. "Follow your heart wherever that may lead you. You need no one's approval…not even Father's." I only came back here to see my mother. I truly regret that I added to her suffering after Theo went, and if there is anything I can do to make it up to her it is my solemn promise that I will.'

'I never sought compensation from you, Ludo. But you have already lifted my heart and my spirits by coming back to me and bringing me a soon-to-be beloved daughter.'

Eva Petrakis pulled him into her arms and hugged him fiercely. Then she moved across to Natalie and gently touched coral-painted fingertips to her cheek. Her pretty blue eyes were moist with tears.

'Not only has my dear son returned to me, but he has brought me the daughter that I have long prayed for. One day I hope she will grant my dearest wish and present me with my first grandchild.'

The sound of birdsong, and in the distance of the waves crashing onto the seashore, faded out to be replaced by an almost dizzying white noise in Natalie's head. She didn't seem to have the ability to feel anything but shock and distress after Ludo's poignant outburst. And now, after what his mother had just said, she hardly trusted herself to string a coherent sentence together. All she knew was that the woman standing in front of her with such hope and trust in her eyes didn't deserve any more heartache or pain. But then neither did her son…

'I think we have stood out here in the midday sun for long enough.' Eva smiled. 'We should all go inside for a while, and I will see to some refreshments for us. I assume you are staying for lunch? But *course* you are! We have so much to celebrate. This is turning out to be a very good day indeed.' Frowning at her husband, who hadn't moved so much as an inch since his son had publically berated him, she said, 'Come with me, Alekos. I think we should have a little talk before we join the children.'

As they moved towards the open patio doors that led inside the house Ludo gripped Natalie's hand hard— as though it were a lifeline in the choppiest of stormy seas. He made a point of deliberately ignoring his father's gaze completely.

CHAPTER TEN

LUDO HAD STAYED ominously quiet so far on the return journey to his villa, and Natalie knew why. Although his mother had tried hard to get the two men to make peace with each other during a delicious prolonged lunch they had both stubbornly resisted her efforts. Ludo was angry with his father for not understanding or forgiving his need to escape after his brother's funeral, and in Natalie's opinion Alekos was holding on to an old perception of his son that he either couldn't or *wouldn't* change.

At any rate, the conversation that had taken place had mostly been between herself and Eva Petrakis, and by the time it had come for the two couples to say their goodbyes father and son were barely even making eye contact.

The situation couldn't have been sadder. After Ludo's impassioned outburst, confessing his feelings, there should have been some resolution between him and his father—or at least a willingness on both their parts to forgive what had happened between them so that they could make some headway into forging a better relationship in the future.

But in spite of her compassion, and her concern for

Ludo's dilemma, Natalie found she couldn't ignore her own needs. She wanted to make it clear to him that she wasn't blindly going to go along with whatever he wanted to make his life easier just because he'd paid her father more for his business. He'd asserted he was no blackmailer, but he *did* have a reputation for ruthlessly winning deals, and she didn't want to end up feeling a fool.

As they drove on towards the villa, Natalie couldn't remain silent any longer. 'I know that the situation at your parents' was very difficult for you,' she told him, nervously clutching her hands together in her lap, 'but it wasn't easy for me either. I can see now why you brought me with you and made that deal with me. It's easier to confront a situation like you have with your father when you have someone else in your corner— someone to help act as a sort of buffer between you. But my big concern is that you're thinking of me purely as one of your business deals, and all you want is the outcome you desire without taking into account *my* feelings.'

She saw Ludo's shoulders tense immediately and his hands firmed on the steering wheel. He momentarily took his eyes off the road to consider her bleakly.

'Is that really the impression you have of me, Natalie? That I only think of you as a business deal I want to win at all costs and don't regard you as a person with needs of your own?'

The surprised and hurt tone in his voice made her anxious that she'd got his motives completely wrong. Her face coloured hotly.

'You *do* regard me, then?' Her voice dropped to a near whisper even as her eyes filled with tears. 'I mean…you do care about what I feel?'

'The fact that you have to ask tells me that you do not think I do. I think it is probably best if we finish this conversation back at the house.'

Scowling, he trained his gaze firmly back on the road, and Natalie turned hers away to stare forlornly out of the window.

It was dusk when they reached the villa. Still quiet, Ludo held the door open for her to precede him. As they entered the spacious open-plan lounge with its sea of marble flooring she was about to speak when he abruptly brushed past her and swept up the marble staircase.

'Ludo, where are you going?'

Because of their conversation in the car, Natalie's felt almost sick with fear that he was going to tell her to go home…that he no longer required her help. She made a snap decision to pursue him, seeing with surprise that he was ripping open the buttons of his linen shirt and taking it off as he went. The arresting sight of his bare, taut, tanned musculature and athletic shoulders sent her heart bumping not only in alarm but with a dizzying sense of excitement too. What on earth was he doing?

Not quick enough to reach him, she saw him get to his bedroom and stride inside without even turning to see if she followed. Taking a deep breath, she cautiously rapped her knuckles against the door. Even though it was partially open she wouldn't risk walking in unannounced.

'Ludo? I know you're probably not in the mood for talking, but you're starting to worry me. I don't want the conversation we had in the car just now to come between us and make us stop communicating. Can I come in?'

'Of course. Unless you want us to converse with each other from either side of the door.'

Smoothing a nervous hand down the front of the blue dress he had professed to like so much, Natalie pushed the door wider and walked inside. Ludo was standing in front of the large silk-canopied bed that dominated the room and seemed to be making a deliberate point of tracking every step of her cautious approach.

'Why did you take off your shirt?' It hadn't been the first thing she wanted to ask him, but she asked anyway because she was curious.

'I wanted to get rid of the taint of disapproval from my father. Unfortunately it's apt to cling and cast a shadow if I keep it on. I didn't want that.'

Even as he discarded the crumpled garment onto the bedspread he glanced at Natalie with a provocative smile. His magnificent sculpted torso was bare, and his rust-coloured chinos were riding low enough on his well-defined lean hips for her to glimpse the column of darker hair that led even lower down. She forced herself not to be so swayed by his arresting male beauty that she wouldn't be able to discuss things sensibly.

'So it's not because I made you angry by asking if you regarded our arrangement as purely a business deal you had to win?'

'It didn't make me angry, but it did upset me coupled with the fact that our reunion lunch with my parents was

spoilt by my father glaring at me across the table like I
was public enemy number one. It's not hard to understand why I'm on edge and would prefer to just forget
about the whole thing.'

'But it won't help if you simply put what happened
to the back of your mind.' Natalie sighed. 'It won't be
as easy to discard as your shirt, Ludo. The memory
will surface again and again if you don't try and deal
with it properly. If you want to talk about it then I'm a
good listener.'

'So you would still listen to my troubles even though
you are suspicious of my motives?'

Her heart twisted with regret that she'd expressed
that. 'I've just had to contend with you telling your parents that you're buying me an engagement ring tomorrow and there will be a wedding in the autumn, when
none of that is remotely true. But now that I've met your
parents and seen how much they mean to you I think
I'm astute enough to know that you mean no harm by
the deception. If you want to talk to me about things
I really am willing to listen and try and help if I can.'

'It might not be true that we're getting married in the
autumn, but I still intend to buy you an engagement ring.
Our engagement will hardly be convincing if I don't. I
take it even if you don't agree you will still keep your
part of the deal?'

Pursing her lips at the suggestion of doubt in his tone,
Natalie nodded her head. 'I will. But right now I'd like
you to open up to me a little and tell me how you *really*
feel about things.'

Ludo scowled. 'You think I'll feel better if I get

things off my chest? Is that what you're saying? Don't you think I've done enough of that today? You saw how my father dealt with it. It only made things even worse between us.'

'He's probably feeling just like you are right now. Instead of feeling justified that he was so stubborn, I bet he wishes he could turn back the clock and have the time over again to make things right. You're his *son*, Ludo. I'm sure he loves you very much.'

The man in front of her was still wearing a mistrustful scowl. 'I don't want to discuss this any further. What I want to do is have a drink. Preferably a *strong* one.' Feeling uncomfortably cornered, he rubbed an irritable hand round his jaw.

'And that's going to solve everything, is it?' Shaking her head in dismay, Natalie frowned. It was quite unbelievable how stubborn he could be. Clearly he must have inherited the trait from his father.

'No. It's not. But it's going to help me feel a hell of a lot better than I do right now after that debacle of a family reunion!'

He dragged the heel of his hand across his chest and his riveting sapphire eyes glistened furiously. But the anger that had appeared as suddenly as a flash flood out of a clear blue sky dispersed just as quickly, and this time his gaze transfixed her for an entirely different reason. It was smouldering with unmistakable *lust*.

'That is,' he drawled, 'unless you can think of another way of making me feel better, Natalie....'

She swore she could count every single beat of her heart as she stood there. In the past few seconds her ability to hear every sound that echoed round that stylish and spacious bedroom, right down to the waves breaking onto the shore outside, had somehow become preternaturally sharp, as had the rest of her senses.

Lifting her hair off the back of her neck to help cool her heated skin, she murmured, 'I can't. But that doesn't mean I want you to drink. Alcohol is what my father resorted to when he couldn't deal with his despair—and take it from me, it only made things worse. Is that what you want, Ludo? To feel worse than you do already? Much better to talk things out than to let your feelings fester and make you ill.'

'It must have been a great boon to your father to have a daughter like you. So wise for someone so young… and so forgiving.'

Natalie felt the heat rising in her cheeks, because she didn't know if he was being sincere or sardonic. 'When you love somebody you naturally want to do everything you can to help them when they need it.'

'I agree. But what if sometimes you need *their* help even more? Do you think that makes you a bad person?'

'Of course not.' Tucking her hair behind her ear with a less than steady hand, she realised that Ludo might have taken her well-meant reply about helping someone you love as a criticism of his own actions when he'd departed after his brother's funeral instead of staying behind to help his parents deal with their grief. She'd be mortified if he believed that. 'Ludo, I hope you don't think I was being insensitive. I was only trying to explain what motivated me to help *my* dad.'

'Is it even possible that someone like you could be insensitive? I don't think so. Come over here.'

'Why?'

He shrugged a shoulder. 'I want to talk to you. I also want to apologise for making you think I don't regard your feelings.'

Gesturing for her to move closer, he gave her a smile that was indisputably slow and seductive. Natalie did as he asked—she couldn't resist him. But her legs were shaking so badly she hardly knew how she managed it.

When they were face to face Ludo lifted his hand and slid it beneath the heavy silken weight of her long hair, letting his palm curve warmly against her nape. His touch and the intimate closeness of his body electrified her into stillness. So much so that her nipples stung with an almost unholy ache for him to touch them. Never before, in all her twenty-four years, had she experienced such wanton, primitive desire for a man—and the force of it shook her hard.

'I said I would only expect you to share my bed if you invited yourself into my room,' he reminded her huskily, his burning blue gaze shamelessly scorching her.

'Is that why you said you wanted to talk to me?' She found herself mesmerised by the alluring sculpted shape of his lips and the heat that reached out to her from his half-naked body. It was impossible to keep her nerves steady.

'Do you know how long I've waited for a girl like you to come into my life?' he asked.

'What do you mean by that? Do you mean you hoped

to meet someone ordinary who doesn't move in the same exalted circles as you do?'

'You are far from ordinary, *glykia mou*…and I don't care where you come from or what kind of circles you move in. I'm simply telling you that I want you.'

'Why?' She barely knew why she even asked, because the answer was shockingly apparent as his eager hands shaped her bottom through her dress and brought her body flush against his. Behind the button fly of his chinos she sensed his heat and his hardness—and he didn't try to hide it to spare her blushes.

'I think there's been enough talking. I'm sure you knew that when you knocked on my door and asked if you could come in…'

A shuddering sigh of need left Natalie's throat as Ludo reached for the zip at the back of her dress, dragged it downwards and stripped the garment off her shoulders. Just when she thought he might be going to kiss her he slid his fingers beneath the straps of the daring black lace bra that she'd bought for this trip, hardly knowing why she should select such an uncharacteristically impractical item. It was a million miles away from her usual safe utilitarian style.

Ludo yanked down the delicate silk and lace to bare her breasts. With a bold glance that challenged her to deny him he cupped her and brought his mouth firmly down onto a stinging erect nipple. His hot wet tongue caressed her flesh and his teeth bit, sending shooting spears of molten lightning straight to her womb. The pleasure-pain was so intense that she grabbed on to his head with a groan. A few sizzling seconds later he looked up and with a devil-may-care glance dragged the rest of her dress down to her feet and helped her step out of it. As Natalie tremblingly kicked off her shoes he kept her steady by holding firmly on to her hips. When she was done, he deftly unhooked her bra and let it fall to the floor.

'Do you know how beautiful you are? You are like a goddess,' he declared, sweeping his gaze appreciatively up and down her semi-nude figure. 'So beautiful that it hurts me to look at you.'

Ludo meant every word. She had the most exquisite shape, highlighted by an impossibly tiny waist and gently flaring hips. And with her river of shining hair cascading down over her pert breasts she reminded him again of mythological depictions of Athena and Andromeda. His attempt to make peace with his father earlier had been anything *but* a success, but being here with Natalie like this, fulfilling the fantasy that he'd been gripped by since first seeing her on the train to London, was going a long way to helping him set aside his personal pain.

Her luminous grey eyes widened as he stooped to position one arm beneath her thighs and the other round her back. The texture of her matchless smooth skin was like the softest velvet, and the experience of holding her semi-naked body in his arms was one of the keenest pleasures he had ever known. With her luxuriant hair brushing tantalisingly against his forearm and the scent of her perfume saturating his senses like a hot and thirsty sirocco, she was a woman to weave serious sexual fantasies about.

But it wasn't just Natalie's looks that made her appeal to him more than any other woman he'd been attracted to before. There was an air of innocence about her that was utterly refreshing after the parade of hard-nosed businesswomen, models and gold-diggers he'd dated from time to time. He'd known his parents would love her…how could they not? She was just the kind of girl they'd always hoped he would meet. And behind his desire, behind the hope he dared not give a name to, there was a nagging sensation of being jealous of any other man who had known her intimately. Had they realised at the time what a prize they'd won for themselves?

Pushing his jealousy aside, he tipped Natalie back and carefully lowered her onto the opulent silk counterpane. As he stood beside the bed, taking the opportunity to survey her loveliness, she returned the compliment by letting her gaze avidly roam him. The hunger in her eyes was unmistakable, and it hardened Ludo even more.

Natalie caught her breath. The well-defined biceps beneath Ludo's naturally bronzed skin intensified the desire that had been building in her blood all day. She was suddenly impatient for him to join her, so that she might know first-hand the raw power that his strong, fit body exuded so effortlessly. The man was temptation personified, and it never failed to strike her how perfectly proportioned and beautiful he was.

As soon as her glance fell into that sea of sapphire-blue once more he gave her a dazzling and knowing smile and dropped down next to her on the bed. The need for conversation redundant, he moved over her with graceful fluidity and straddled her hips with his strong, long-boned thighs. When he sat back on his haunches to undo his chinos her ability to think clearly utterly fled. All Natalie knew was that she wanted Ludo as much as he wanted her—if not *more*. Yet she momentarily closed her eyes when he dispensed with his trousers and the navy silk boxers that he wore underneath simply because she couldn't stem her anxiety over not being able to please him as much as a man of his experience might be expecting her to...

How could she when she'd never gone all the way with a man before?

Would he be furious with her when he found out? She'd long realised she must be in quite a minority to be still a virgin at twenty-four.

Her nervousness immediately evaporated the instant Ludo touched his lips to hers. The man's deliciously expert kisses were to *die* for. When she responded eagerly, her own lack of expertise didn't seem to matter one iota. Winding her arms about his strong neck, she gave herself up to the passionate embrace with all her heart, and didn't tense when he caught the sides of her lace panties and rolled them down over her thighs. The only feelings that washed though her right then were excitement and lust, and when he returned to claim her mouth in another avaricious kiss Natalie couldn't help but wind her long slender legs round his hard, lean waist. It all seemed so natural and so right.

'Let me love you,' he entreated against her ear, murmuring low.

With her hands resting on the strong banks of his

shoulders, she gave him a tremulous smile. 'There is nothing I want more,' she admitted softly.

Somewhere along the line he had retrieved a foil packet from his trouser pocket and he briefly sat back on his haunches to deal with protection. But not before Natalie allowed herself a curious glimpse. With a contented sigh she rested her head back on the sumptuous silk pillow and readied herself to receive him.

She bit down hard on her lip at his first eager invasion, and couldn't deny the initial sting of pain that she experienced—but when Ludo's muscular body suddenly stilled in surprise she pulled him against her to encourage him to continue, kissing him. There would be plenty of time for that particular awkward discussion later, she thought. Right now all Natalie wanted was to be made love to by the man she now knew without a doubt was the thief of her heart. A man who on the surface appeared to have everything that was supposed to signal success in the world…wealth, property, business acumen second to none, as well as movie-star good looks.

But in truth, she reflected, he was clearly lacking the one thing he perhaps craved above all else—the thing most people yearned for. Unconditional love and acceptance. From family, friends and colleagues, and—given time—*the person they fell in love with.* Even though that last part of her realisation made her pulse race, Natalie knew she wouldn't deny her lover anything. Not now, when she'd just surrendered her most precious gift to him.

Pressing himself deeper and deeper inside her, Ludo wound his fingers through hers as they began to move as one, his breathing becoming more and more laboured as he succumbed fully to the passion that drove him so hungrily to seek release.

For Natalie, the tide of molten heat that had consumed her from the moment he'd welcomed her into his room was now at its peak, and the power of it was like a ferocious drowning sea, sweeping her away to a heart-pounding place of no return...

Wrapping her in his arms as he lay spent beside her, Ludo felt his mind teeming with questions. His heart thudding, he lightly twined a long strand of her silken hair round his fingers and asked, 'Why didn't you tell me that this would be your first time?'

Meeting his glance with her big grey eyes, Natalie gave him a long, considered look. 'Would you have still made love to me if I'd admitted it?'

'You are far too irresistible for me *not* to have. But I would have tried to be a little more gentle...more considerate.'

'I loved it that you were so passionate, Ludo. I may not have much experience, but even so I have desires—just like you.'

His heart thudded a little less hard but he was still confounded by her frank response. Confounded and enthralled. He'd never met a woman like her. 'What made you wait so long to give yourself to someone?'

She blushed, and because she looked so adorable Ludo couldn't help planting a light kiss on her forehead.

'My mother always told me to wait until the time was right...until I was sure that the man I gave my virginity to was worthy of it. Well, today was the day I knew the time was right and the man more than worthy.'

'See what you've done, my angel?'

'What do you mean? What have I done?'

'You have made me want you all over again.'

With a shameless grin, Ludo impelled her firmly onto his aroused manhood, proud and pleased that she fitted him like the most exquisite satin glove.

'Except this time, although I will be no less passionate, I will endeavour to go more slowly...to take my time and savour you more so that you may experience the utmost pleasure.'

Her long hair cascaded down over her naked breasts like a waterfall and her beautiful eyes widened to saucers. 'Like lessons in love, you mean?'

With a throaty laugh of sheer delight, he stilled any further inclination she might have to talk by capturing her lips in a long and sexy, heartfelt kiss...

CHAPTER ELEVEN

EVEN THOUGH THE afternoon at his parents' had not gone as well as he might have dared to hope, it had been one of the most wonderful evenings of his life. Natalie had Ludo in a spin. The air of innocence that he'd sensed about her from the beginning had been proved to be right. But he was stunned at just how far that innocence had extended. More than that, at the fact that she would willingly surrender that innocence to *him*. In spite of the upsetting altercation with his father earlier, he was walking on air—and predisposed to take his lover out to dinner.

He no longer cared that the locals would see him and know that he'd returned, or indeed if they made private unflattering judgements about him. It was strange, but with Natalie by his side Ludo felt as if he could deal with just about *anything*—even the painful realisation that he would probably never have his father's love and regard.

His favourite local restaurant overlooking the moonlit bay was heaving with tourists and locals alike tonight, and as soon as he and Natalie walked in heads turned to observe them. Deciding it was because his partner looked so ravishing in her mint-coloured dress and the cream pashmina that she'd draped round her shoulders, Ludo felt a strong glow of pride eddy through him.

'*Kopiaste*...welcome. Come in and join us,' the restaurant staff eagerly greeted them. Accustomed to getting a table wherever he went, whether he'd booked ahead or not, Ludo decided not to go elsewhere when he was told they were fully booked tonight but would not dream of turning him and his beautiful partner away. He smilingly kept hold of Natalie's hand and waited patiently while a space in one of the most attractive parts of the restaurant was hastily made available and an extra table was laid. The friendly *maître d'*, whose family Ludo had known for years, attended them personally, and on his instruction a young waiter and waitress brought appetising plates of *mezes* and some complimentary *ouzo* to their table in celebration of his return home.

But although the staff behaved impeccably Ludo could see in their eyes that they were having difficulty containing their curiosity. He had read the speculation in the Greek press three years ago about why he'd left the country so abruptly following his brother's funeral. The picture they'd painted of him had not been a good one...

'Everybody seems so pleased to see you,' Natalie commented, her grey eyes shining.

'Of course.' Ludo couldn't help being wry. 'Money talks.'

'Please don't be cynical. Not tonight. I'm feeling so happy and I want to stay feeling that way...at least until the evening is over.'

Reaching for her small elegant hand, he could have bitten off his tongue for bringing that wounded look to her eyes. 'I fear my cynicism about people has become a habit. But it doesn't mean that can't change,' he added, smiling.

'No, it doesn't,' she agreed and, lifting his hand, brushed her soft lips across his knuckles.

'You are a dangerous woman, Natalie Carr,' he responded, deliberately lowering his voice. 'A small kiss and one approving glance from your bewitching grey eyes and I'm undone. All I really want to do now is take you home and teach you some more lessons in love.'

Her pretty cheeks coloured, just as Ludo had known they would.

'Well…I know I have a lot to learn. But, as tempting as that sounds, I'd really like something to eat first. What do you recommend?'

He didn't even bother to glance at the leather-bound menu he'd been given. He knew it like the back of his hand. There had been many occasions in the past when he and his brother Theo had dined here. He deliberately set the heartrending memory aside to concentrate on Natalie.

'Leave it to me.' He smiled, and immediately signalled for the *maître d',* who had made sure to stay close by in readiness to take his order.

That night Natalie fell asleep in Ludo's arms, with the sweet scent of night-blooming jasmine drifting in through the open windows of the bedroom. It seemed that everything that had happened was taking on the magical qualities of a dream, and she wished that life might imitate that dream forever.

When she woke early the next morning, with her head on Ludo's chest, Natalie couldn't resist spending several minutes just breathing in his unique warm scent and observing the handsome features that looked more peaceful and vulnerable than she'd ever seen them. There was nothing remotely threatening or untrustworthy about him, she concluded. He had a good heart. Why couldn't his father see that? She refused to believe her perception was coloured rose just because she only saw the good in Ludo, and because she was head over heels in love with him.

Hugging herself at the reason why she suddenly felt so light and free, she planted the softest kiss on the blade of his chiselled jaw and regretfully left the lavish warm bed. Leaving him to sleep on, she dressed in a pair of light blue denims and a white cotton shirt, then made her way downstairs in search of some coffee and perhaps some delicious Greek bread to go with it. Making love certainly built up an appetite, she thought. She was absolutely starving!

She was drinking her second cup of coffee, courtesy of Allena, when Ludo walked out onto the patio to find her. He too was wearing jeans, but with an ice-blue shirt that emphasised the stunning hue of his incredible eyes. She noticed that he hadn't had a shave, and his jaw was shadowed with bristles. There was no question that it suited him. The less groomed look made him appear dangerous and sexy as hell, Natalie decided, the tips of her breasts tingling fiercely at the delicious memory of his ardent lovemaking last night…

'Good morning,' she said with a smile, her hands curved round her still steaming cup of coffee.

'Kalimera.' He strode round the table and with a grin removed the cup of coffee and put it down on the table. Then he gently but firmly hauled her to her feet. 'I was worried when I woke up and found you gone,' he intoned huskily, moving her body intimately close to his.

'There was no need. I only came down here for a cup of coffee and some bread. My appetite is at its sharpest in the morning.'

'Really? Then why did you desert me? I would have willingly satisfied your hunger if you'd stayed in bed with me.'

Feeling as though she'd strayed to the edge of a cliff and was about to plunge headlong over the precipice, Natalie dug her fingers into Ludo's hard lean waist as if her life depended on it. 'You're a very bad boy,' she said softly, unable to help the slight quaver in her voice.

He lifted an amused eyebrow. 'If I'm bad, it's because you're always tempting me, Miss Carr. Promise me you'll never stop being the one temptation I can never resist?'

He kissed her hard, angling her jaw so that he could deepen the scalding contact even more. Natalie was dizzy with desire and longing for him. Her blood pounded hotly through her veins as though she was on fire. When he laid his hand over her breast beneath her shirt she couldn't help wishing with all her heart that she had indeed stayed in bed with him this morning, instead of leaving him to go in search of coffee.

'Excuse me, Mr Petrakis, your father is here to see you.'

Allena's slightly nervous but respectful voice had them both turning abruptly in shock and surprise. Ludo's features suddenly turned unnaturally pale. With his blue eyes briefly conveying a silent apology, he moved away from Natalie to go and stand in front of his housekeeper.

'Where is he?' he asked her.

Allena told him that she'd taken him into the living room and was about to make him some coffee.

'Tell him I'll join him in a minute.'

When Allena had returned inside Natalie went straight over to Ludo and instinctively reached for his hand. He flinched as though abruptly woken from a dream. It was easy to see that this unexpected turn of events had caught him on the raw, and she wondered what he was thinking.

'Are you all right?'

'Not really.' He freed his hand from hers to drag his fingers through the already mussed golden strands of his hair. 'Whatever he wants to say to me, it can't be good.'

'You don't know that yet. Why don't you just go in and talk to him, help put your mind at rest, instead of standing out here worrying?'

He scowled, already turning away from her. 'Like I said, whatever he has to say to me, it can't be good. It never is. Go and finish your coffee, Natalie. No doubt I'll be back soon.'

She watched him go as though he were about to present himself in front of a firing squad, and silently prayed that whatever Alekos Petrakis had to say to his son it wouldn't make him despise himself even more than he already did over the tragic events of three years ago.

His father had his back to him when Ludo entered the living room, and he realised that he was twisting and turning a long string of tasselled orange marble worry beads known as *komboloi* that had been passed on to him by his own father when he was young. The sight jolted him into stillness for a moment. It had been a long time since he'd seen him use them. The last time had been at his brother's funeral.

Sucking in a deep breath to steady himself, he announced his arrival with, 'Hello, Father. You want to see me?'

The older man hastily slid the beads into the pocket of his immaculate suit jacket and turned round. Once again it shocked Ludo to see the deep new lines of worry that furrowed his brow.

'Ludovic. You were not about to go out, I trust?'

'Not immediately, no.' Ludo did indeed have plans for himself and Natalie that morning, but it wouldn't hurt to delay them.

'Good. Shall we sit down? I believe that your excellent housekeeper is bringing some coffee.'

They moved across the room to the two lavish gold couches positioned either side of a carved mahogany table. Almost right on cue Allena appeared with a tray of coffee and a dish of small *baklavas*. Thanking her,

Ludo reached forward to hand his father a cup and saucer and poured him his beverage. It was such a simple, commonplace gesture, but somehow he had a sense that it had more significance than he perhaps realised.

Stirring a generous spoonful of sugar into his coffee, Alekos asked, 'Where is your charming fiancée this morning?'

'She's waiting for me outside on the patio.'

'As much as it would please me to have her join us, I think it best that she does not. At least not until we have had some private time together...do you agree?'

Taken aback that his father would even *consider* his opinion, Ludo lightly shrugged a shoulder. 'I agree. There is no point in including her in our conversation if things are going to be unpleasant.'

Alekos Petrakis gravely shook his head, as if he couldn't quite believe what he had just heard. 'Am I such an ogre that you automatically expect things to be *unpleasant* between us? If you do, then all I can tell you is that I truly regret that.'

Stunned into silence, Ludo watched him wipe away the tear that had trickled down over his weathered bronzed cheek. Never before had he known his father to weep, or indeed to be sentimental in any way. What on earth was going on?

'You had better tell me what you want to say, Father. I'm sure you must have some particular reason for coming here to see me today.'

Returning his cup and saucer to the table, Alekos Petrakis sighed heavily and linked his hands together across his lap. 'I came here to tell you that I love you, my son. And to express my deep regret that for all these years you did not know it. Your mother and I had a long talk last night after your visit, and she made me see how foolish and stubborn I have been…how *blind* I have been about you. It was fear that made me that way. Fear of losing you.'

His mouth drying, Ludo stared. 'What do you mean, fear of losing me?'

Alekos's dark eyes met and cleaved to his. 'We have never told you, but you were born premature and we nearly lost you. The doctors worked day and night to save your life. One day our hopes would be high that you were going to survive, and the next…' After a helpless catch in his voice he made himself continue. 'The next day we'd prepare ourselves to bury you. We were told by the doctors that even if you lived you would never be strong. When you did survive, and we brought you home, your poor mother watched over you day and night like a hawk, and I somehow convinced myself that it was *my* fault you were so weak…that I had in me bad seed. What other reason could there be? Theo was big and strong—why weren't you?'

Rising to his feet, Alekos pulled out a handkerchief to mop his brow. 'My logic was ridiculous. I see that now. Your mother always told me that Theo might be the big and strong son but you—*you* were the hand-some and clever one. I wish I had seen that when you were a boy, Ludovic, because your mother turned out to be absolutely right. But whether you are handsome and clever, or big and strong, it does not matter. What matters is that you know I am proud of you and love you as deeply and strongly as I loved your dear brother. Can you forgive a very foolish old man for the stupidity of the past so that he may build a happier relationship with his beloved son in the future?'

Already on his feet, Ludo strode round the table and embraced his father hard. It was as though the dam that had been closed against the forceful sea of emotion behind the gates of his heart had suddenly burst open, and the relief it brought made him feel as if he could breathe freely again.

'There is nothing to forgive, Father. I too have made a grave mistake in believing that you didn't care for me as much as you did my brother. I also have a stubborn streak, and sometimes believe I am right when I am wrong. I deeply regret walking away after Theo died. I convinced myself that you had no time for me, that my achievements were not as worthy of regard as his were, and that if I stayed it would be like rubbing salt into the wound of losing him.'

'He would be cross with us both for being so stubborn and wasting so much time in feeling aggrieved, no?'

Grinning, Ludo stepped out of the embrace and slapped his father on the back. 'He would. But he'd also be happy that we have at last made amends. So will my mother when you tell her. Nothing would make me happier than knowing that she feels more at peace about our relationship.'

'I have a question for you,' said Ludo's father.

'What's that?' Old habits died hard, and Ludo

couldn't help tensing a little in anticipation of what he was going to ask.

'I wanted to ask you about Margaritari…your island. What do you intend to do about it now? It has been a long time since you have allowed people to stay on it, and it seems such a shame to leave such a beautiful place to lay in waste when it could bring people pleasure. Nor should you let what happened to Theo destroy your own pleasure in it, Ludo.'

'I admit that I've missed visiting the island. It is like no other place on earth. When we visited it as children Theo and I knew it was special. That's why as soon as I had the chance I bought it.'

His father looked thoughtful. 'Then go and visit it again. Take Natalie and go and create some happy memories there to alleviate the sorrowful ones. For what it's worth, my son, I really think you should take my advice.'

Ludo thought he should, too. But first there was something important he had to do…something that involved purchasing an engagement ring.

As if reading his mind, Alekos put his arm round his shoulders and said, 'Now, let us go and find your beautiful fiancée. I want to reassure her that you and I no longer bear any grudges. I also want to tell her that I am proud my son has been guided by his heart and not his head in choosing such a lovely woman to be his wife. Which reminds me—weren't you two supposed to be getting an engagement ring today?'

Not missing a beat, Ludo replied, 'We were—we *are*.'

'Good. Then later on tonight we must meet up again,

so that your mother and I can see the ring, and then go out to dinner and celebrate.'

Natalie was over the moon when Ludo appeared with his father and they told her that all previous tensions or grudges between them were no more. Following the wonderful revelation that both men were now willing to forgive and forget, she made the discovery over more coffee and *baklava* that Alekos Petrakis had a wicked sense of humour as he regaled her with illuminating tales from his boyhood and the mischief he had got up to.

'I was not always the upstanding citizen you see before you today!' he confessed laughingly.

But even as she enjoyed his jokes and stories Natalie couldn't help feeling a little down. It was clear that Alekos was regarding her as his son's *bona fide* wife-to-be, and yet again she couldn't help feeling hurt because it wasn't true. How would he and his charming wife Eva react when they found out that her engagement to Ludo was nothing but a sham? That as soon as they left Greece in all probability she'd be going back to work in the bed and breakfast she ran with her mother, never to see their charismatic son again…even though in secret she loved him with all her heart?

When Alekos had bade them goodbye, making them promise they would drive over that evening to show them the engagement ring they had chosen, Natalie felt almost sick with guilt and regret.

In complete contrast to the blues that had descended on *her*, Ludo was uncharacteristically relaxed and happy. 'Will you do something for me?' he asked, impelling her into his arms as they returned inside the house after waving his father goodbye.

Her nerves jangled a little and her mouth dried. Her gaze was wary. 'What's that?'

His blue eyes sparkling, as though nothing was amiss or possibly *could* be, he replied, 'I want you to go upstairs and find something pretty to wear. Perhaps the beautiful dress you wore on our first night here? I'd like to get some photographs of us together when we buy the engagement ring.'

Natalie blinked and stared. 'Don't you think this charade has gone far enough, Ludo?'

'I don't know what you mean.'

'Are you honestly saying you want to keep up the pretence that we're engaged? It's going to break your father's heart when he learns that it's not true, and, personally, I *really* don't want to be responsible for that. He's a good man, and you've just made up with him after years of hardly speaking to each other. How do you think he's going to feel when he finds out you've been playing him for a fool?'

His hands dropping away from her waist as if he'd been mortally stung, Ludo flashed her a piercing blue gaze like the precursor to an all-out thunderstorm.

'Again I have to ask you—have you forgotten the deal we made before we flew out here?'

Her heart knocking painfully against her ribs, Natalie shook her head sadly. 'I've forgotten nothing, Ludo... including giving you my word that I'd pretend to be your fiancée unless things became too difficult or untenable.

I have to tell you that that's exactly what they've become. *Untenable.*'

With her head held high and her heart pierced by unbearable sorrow, she headed for the marble staircase without sparing him a second glance.

CHAPTER TWELVE

THE BEDROOM DOOR was flung open just as Natalie was hauling her suitcase onto the bed in order to pack. With the heel of her hand she hastily scrubbed away the scalding tears that had been blurring her vision and spun round to find Ludo standing in the doorway, with his arms crossed over his chest and an enigmatic smile hitching his lips.

She was immediately incensed. 'I can't believe you think the situation is remotely amusing! The fact that you do tells me you're not the man I thought you were.'

'I am far from amused that you think my father too good a man to be deceived about our engagement. Anything *but*.'

'Then what are you smiling about?'

Inside her chest Natalie's heart ached with distress. All she wanted to do right now was board the next plane back to the UK and spend some time reflecting on what she could do to prevent herself from ever being so gullible again.

Slowly, Ludo started to walk across the room towards her. When he was almost a foot away Natalie caught the familiar sensuous drift of his cologne and her insides cartwheeled. How would she ever come to terms with not seeing him again? Her feelings for him were no five-minute wonder, here today and gone tomorrow, she was crazy about him—despite his using her to help achieve his own ends. It didn't matter that he'd made a deal with her, or that he'd followed through on his part of the bargain—she now found she couldn't meet hers. How could she when even contemplating such a painful idea had suddenly become impossible?

'You've been crying,' he observed.

There was a look in his eyes that momentarily stole her breath.

'Yes, I've been crying.' Sniffing, she pulled out a crumpled tissue from her jeans pocket and blew her nose.

'Why?'

'Can't you guess? I'm crying because you were right, Ludo…it *is* going to break my heart to leave you. I also don't want to leave Greece. I didn't want to go home so soon, but now I'm going to have to. I thought I could do this but I can't…not after learning how much it means to your mother that you've met someone special and are engaged, and not after listening to your father today and seeing how much he loves you. I can't do it because I'm not mercenary and I don't want to hurt people. If you want to sue me for reneging on our deal then go ahead. There's nothing I can do about that.'

'You said that it would break your heart to leave me. Did you mean it?'

Sounding amazed, Ludo moved in a little closer and

smiled. Feeling heat pour into her face, Natalie swallowed hard and stared.

'Yes. I'm not trying to put you in an awkward position, but I mean it.'

'How does telling me such an incredible thing put me in an awkward position?

'I don't want you to feel you have to do anything about it. It's bad enough that people are going to be hurt because I'm not going to be able to continue to carry out my part of our bargain.'

'You mean my parents?' His expression was grave.

'Of course I mean your parents'

'What about me, Natalie? Do you not consider that I might be hurt if you don't adhere to our bargain and agree to be my fiancée?'

'You mean if I don't *pretend* to be your fiancée?'

'I no longer want you to pretend.'

He moved in even closer—so close that his warm breath fanned her face. Every plane and facet of the handsome features that were so dear to her made her heart ache anew, because after today she might never see them again.

Then, suddenly registering what he had just said, she turned rigid with shock. 'What did you say?'

'I said I no longer want you to pretend to be my fiancée. I want us to get engaged for real.'

'You're joking.'

'No, I'm not. I want us to become officially engaged with a view to getting married. I'm deadly serious.'

At the end of this declaration he tenderly gathered Natalie's face between his hands and brought his lips passionately down on hers. There was nothing she could do but eagerly respond. The lessons in love that he had given her had made her an addict for his touch, for the slow, tantalising kisses that rendered her so weak with need that she couldn't think straight…couldn't even remember her own name when he made love to her.

She was so glad his arms were round her waist when she could finally bear to tear her lips away from his or she might have stumbled.

'This really isn't some kind of a joke, is it?' she asked huskily, staring up into the incandescent sea of blue that never failed to mesmerise her.

'No. It isn't a joke. I would never be so cruel. I mean every word I've said. I don't want a pretend engagement, Natalie, I want a real one. So there is no longer any need for you to worry about deceiving my parents. I genuinely want you to be my wife, *agape mou*. When I buy an engagement ring for you today I want it to be for real.'

'But why would you want that?'

'Do you really need to ask? Have you not already guessed?' He exhaled a wry breath, then, smiling warmly down into her eyes, said, 'I love you Natalie… I love you with all my heart and soul and I don't think I can even bear the thought of living without you. That's why I want to marry you.'

For several heart-pounding seconds his passionate declaration stunned her into silence. Then, gathering her wits, she tenderly touched her palm to his cheek and smiled back.

'I love you too, Ludo. I wouldn't consider marrying

you if I didn't. You swept into my life like a whirlwind and turned everything I thought about myself and what I wanted upside down. I know it might sound ridiculous, but I had more or less resigned myself to being single for the rest of my life, because I couldn't imagine marrying anyone for anything less than true love.'

'That is what I thought, too. I longed to find someone real and true who would be my friend and my companion as well as my lover... The idea that a woman might only marry me for my money was a genuine fear of mine.'

'I would never marry you for your money, Ludo.' Natalie frowned. 'I'm an old-fashioned girl who believes that there's someone for everyone—that when two people fall in love it's written in stars.' Her cheeks reddened self-consciously. 'And I believe it was written in the stars that day we met on the train and you paid for my ticket. Especially when you turned out to be the man who was buying my father's business! People sometimes read me wrong because I have a side to me that's very pragmatic, but I've had to be. When my dad left I had to be a support and friend to my mother, as well as help her to get a business up and running so that we had an income. But I'm still an incurable romantic. Anyway, I learned early on in my life, from what happened with my parents, that money is no guarantee of living happily ever after with someone. Not unless their love for each other is more important than anything material.'

Tipping up her chin, Ludo stole a brief, hungry kiss. When he lifted his head to gauge her reaction, he seemed delighted by the fact that she was blushing again.

'I told you once that you have a very sexy voice, remember? As much as I would love to listen to you talk some more, *glykia mou*, we have a special appointment at my friend's jewellers in Lindos. He is closing the shop for the afternoon so that we might take our time in choosing a ring. He is the most sought-after designer and will create something utterly exquisite for you. That may take a few weeks, and we will have to wait for it to be made, but my intention is to buy you a beautiful ring that we can take with us today, so that the world knows we intend to marry. That being the case—we should be making our way over there now.'

'That seems awfully expensive, Ludo. Surely just one ring will do?'

He stole another kiss and playfully pinched her cheek. 'In the circles I've moved in you are unlike any other woman I have ever known, my love. Most of those women have their eye on a man who can keep them in the style they believe they deserve, and they do not much care if he is a good person or even if they really like him…as long as he is rich. But with you, Natalie, I already know you love me for myself and not for the material things I may provide. Therefore I'd be pleased if you indulge me in this matter today.'

'If it means that much to you, then I will.'

'Good.'

'Ludo, can I ask you something? Something we haven't really talked about?'

His hands resting lightly on her hips, he gave her a briefly wary nod. 'What's on your mind?'

Because it wasn't an easy question to ask, and she was slightly dreading hearing the answer, Natalie grimaced. 'Have you—have you had many lovers before me?'

'No. Not many. So few, in fact, that none of them are even memorable. They weren't exactly good choices. But I'm not interested in revisiting my past, Natalie.' He sighed. 'I'm much more interested in what's going on right now and the lovely woman who is standing in front of me...the woman who has so miraculously told me that she loves me and that it would break her heart to leave me.'

'It's true.' It was her turn to reach up and plant a soft kiss on his bristled cheekbone. 'She *does* love you, Ludo...with all her heart. And if you really want a photograph of us to mark the occasion of our engagement I'll go and put on that dress you like so much and tidy my hair.'

'Natalie?'

'Yes?'

'Do you mind going into the bathroom to dress instead of staying in here? Because if you stand here and disrobe I might not be able to resist the temptation to help you.'

'If you do that we'll never get to the jewellers today.'

'You are right. We had better focus on the matter in hand. I'm sure there'll be plenty of time later for the other things I'd like to focus on.'

With a boldly lascivious gleam in the sapphire eyes

she had so come to love, Ludo reluctantly freed her from
his embrace, turned her round and gave her a little push
in the small of her back. He was still chuckling when
she hurried into the bathroom and shut the door.

The heavily perfumed air was just as hypnotic and spell-
binding as Ludo remembered, and it throbbed with the
soporific sound of bees and insects. Blessedly devoid
of the noise of traffic—there was none on the island,
and the only means of reaching it was by boat—if there
was one place in all the world where a person couldn't
help but relax and unwind from day-to-day stresses then
Margaritari was that place.

He'd taken his father's advice about returning to the
island and creating some happier memories, and had
brought Natalie with him to do just that. He had also
shared with his father his conviction that he felt he'd become a better man for having met and fallen in love with
her, and hoped with all his heart that they would enjoy
a marriage as long and as happy as Eva's and Alekos's.

Barefoot, he started to follow the crescent-shaped
arc of lush golden sand, thoughtfully gazing out at the
calm blue waters gently rippling beside it and sending
up a silent prayer of thanks for his good fortune. He
had made his peace with his father and he was in love
with the kindest, most beautiful girl in the world. And
he didn't care who knew it.

Right now Natalie was back in the simple but elegant
stone cottage he'd had built for his own use, telephoning
her father. He hadn't forgotten that his cultural tradition
demanded that he ask him for her hand in marriage, but

first Natalie wanted to talk to Bill Carr in private and tell him why she wanted to marry Ludo. They were madly in love…it was as simple as that.

He hoped her father would not try and talk her out of it in the belief that he was leading her on…that he might not follow through on his declaration to marry her…that he was untrustworthy. Snapping himself out of the old habit of fearing he was not as well regarded as others, he stopped walking and stood quietly staring out to sea at the vast incandescent horizon that stretched out before him. Sadly he remembered his brother Theo. Even though he had died too young, and so tragically, somehow Ludo knew that he was pleased he had made up with their father and had met Natalie and fallen in love with her. He had a strong sense that his beloved brother wished them well…

'Ludo!'

He turned at the sound of the voice that thrilled him like no other, his heart thrumming in anticipation of what she might be going to tell him. He prayed the news was good.

Natalie was running towards him across the sand, barefoot and beautiful in the mint-coloured sarong he had bought her at the market in Lindos, her lovely long hair cascading over her shoulders like a shining water-fall. In her hand she was carrying a small bunch of ole-ander and lavender. As she drew level he made himself resist taking her into his arms and gave her the chance to get her breath back first.

'He gives us both his blessing, and says that you can ring him when we get back to the cottage.' Her grey eyes shining, she grinned. 'He also said I'm to tell you that you're a lucky man…a *very* lucky man.'

'Does he think I don't know that already?' Impatient to hold her, Ludo hauled his wife-to-be against his chest, the heady scent of the small floral bouquet she held drifting hypnotically beneath his nose. 'So, he gives us his blessing and does not mind that you are to become Mrs Ludo Petrakis?'

'As long as it's what I want, then he's more than happy. In fact he's going round to my mum's tomorrow to tell her the news himself. Apparently she's invited him to stay for dinner.' Natalie's brow furrowed a little. 'I suppose it's good that they're talking properly… Anyway, my dad says it's only right that if he gives us his blessing to be married he should be the one to tell her.'

'He sounds to be in good spirits. Is his health any better?'

'Much. You have no idea how much it helped him when you agreed to pay him that extra sum for the business. He says he's buzzing with ideas for a new one. I just hope he doesn't get too carried away and overdo it.'

'And why have you brought these flowers to the beach, *agape mou?* If you want to admire them they are all around us in the coves and by the rock pools… the garden is also full of them.'

'I know. That's where I picked these from. To tell you the truth, I wanted us to say a little prayer for your brother and cast them out to sea in his memory,' Natalie answered softly. 'Do you mind…?'

'Do I *mind*?' Ludo shook his head from side to side in wonderment. 'It is so like you to think of something like this. I'm so proud to know you, Natalie...and prouder still that you are soon to be my wife.'

'Let's do it, then.' Gazing lovingly up into his eyes, she gently stepped out of their embrace and crouched down beside the seashore.

He willingly dropped down beside her. 'Let us remember Theo Petrakis...'

Quietly murmuring a prayer in Greek, Ludo repeated it for Natalie afterwards in English. When he was done, he gestured to her to let her know, and one by one she let the delicate flowers float out into the ocean....

Being on the island was like being on honeymoon. Every night, after making passionate love with the man she loved, Natalie would fall into a blissful sleep in his arms, and every morning, soon after waking, she'd run down to the sea to take a refreshing dip in cool tranquil waters not yet warmed by the sun. Then she'd hurry back to the cottage to have breakfast with Ludo out on the terrace.

They had been on the island for almost a week now, and he had lost that wary look that conveyed his cynicism about the world—a look he'd seemed to wear habitually when they'd first met. He was looking younger every day. Even his brow was less furrowed, as if all his cares had fallen away. Natalie couldn't help but sigh contentedly.

Sitting opposite her at the rattan table, Ludo lowered his aviator sunglasses and his sublime sapphire eyes couldn't help but dazzle her.

'What is it?' he wanted to know.

'I was just thinking how much more relaxed you look than you did when we first met. It must be this place. It's magical, isn't it?'

'There is definitely a touch of paradise about it. I almost have to pinch myself when I remember that I own it.' Straightening in his chair, he tunnelled his fingers through his hair, as if coming to some momentous decision. 'In fact, it is so like paradise that I have decided it's not right to keep it just for myself and family and friends. I've been thinking about building some more accommodation, so that the families of sick children on the surrounding islands might come here for a rest or a holiday when they need it. Of course they wouldn't have to pay for the privilege. I thought I could set up a foundation in Theo's name. What do you think?'

'What do I *think*?' Natalie's heart was racing with excitement and pride. 'I think it's a wonderful idea. Could I help you set it up? If I'm not going to be working at the bed and breakfast any more after we're married I'd like something useful to do…something that I could believe in.'

'Of course you can help. That is…until we have our first child. I'm a strong believer in a mother being there for her children as they are growing up if she can be. How do you feel about that, *glykia mou*?'

'I agree.' Reaching across the table, she smilingly squeezed his hand. 'I want to be there for *all* our children as they grow up. As long as their father is there for them as much as possible, too.'

With a delighted smile, Ludo raised her hand and turned it over to plant a lingering warm kiss in the centre of her palm. 'We very definitely have an agreement. You said *all* our children? That implies we will have more than one or two?'

Natalie dimpled. 'I was thinking maybe three or four?'

'And I'm thinking I'm going to be a very busy man for the next few years if you are planning *that* kind of agenda, my angel. In which case I suppose there's no time like the present to get started on carrying it out!'

* * * * *

A sneaky peek at next month...

MODERN™

INTERNATIONAL AFFAIRS, SEDUCTION & PASSION GUARANTEED

My wish list for next month's titles...

In stores from 19th July 2013:

❏ The Billionaire's Trophy — Lynne Graham

❏ A Royal Without Rules — Caitlin Crews

❏ Imprisoned by a Vow — Annie West

❏ Duty at What Cost? — Michelle Conder

❏ The Rings That Bind — Michelle Smart

In stores from 2nd August 2013:

❏ Prince of Secrets — Lucy Monroe

❏ A Deal with Di Capua — Cathy Williams

❏ Exquisite Acquisitions — Charlene Sands

❏ Faking It to Making It — Ally Blake

❏ First Time For Everything — Aimee Carson

Special Offers

very month we put together collections and
nger reads written by your favourite authors.

ere are some of next month's highlights—
nd don't miss our fabulous discount online!

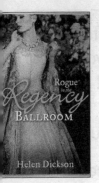

Rogue *in the* **Regency** BALLROOM

Helen Dickson

n sale 2nd August

THE CORRETTIS Scandals

CAITLIN CREWS
MAISEY YATES

On sale 2nd August

PENNY JORDAN

THE SCANDALOUS *Warehams*

On sale 19th July

Save 20%
on all Special Releases